Searching for the Nude in the Landscape

Searching for the Nude in the Landscape

Byrna Barclay

Thistledown Press Ltd.

© Byrna Barclay, 1996
All rights reserved

Canadian Cataloguing in Publication Data

Barclay, Byrna

Searching for the nude in the landscape
ISBN 1-895449-57-X

I. Title.

PS8553.A7618S43 1996   C813'.54   C96-920056-0
PR9199.3.B273S43 1996

Book design by A.M. Forrie
Cover art by Keith Whitcher
Set in 11 pt Original Garamond
by Thistledown Press

Printed and bound in Canada
by Veilleux Printing
Boucherville, Quebec

Thistledown Press Ltd.
633 Main Street
Saskatoon, Saskatchewan
S7H 0J8

Thistledown Press acknowledges the support received for its publishing program
from the Saskatchewan Arts Board and the Canada Council's Block Grants program.

I wish to thank Leon Rooke who sent me from the Saskatchewan School of the Arts in 1984 beyond the borders of my own province and the old boundaries of fiction and poetry. Without my husband, Ron, the frequent flyer, I couldn't have heard these story-songs in Provence and the Caribbean. Without the soul-sustaining Poets' Combine — Judy Krause, Bob Currie, Gary Hyland, Paul Wilson and Bruce Rice — I would have nothing to do the first Friday of every month. I rely, too, on the perception of Pat Krause, the poetic vision of Brenda Niskala, the quick critical wit of Dave Margoshes; my prose group: Three Babes & Dave. And thanks, too, to Thistledown for heeding my call for the visionary Irish songster and devil-of-an-editor, Seán Virgo, whose ancestors drove mine from Ireland in the 12th C, but it took them two hundred years to do it.

ACKNOWLEDGEMENTS

These stories in this collection have been previously published:

"Linnaea, My Twinflower" and "Mirror, Mirror?" as "Seeing Double" in *Fiddlehead* and in *Snapshots: The New Canadian Fiction*, edited by Kristina Russelo, Black Moss Press.
"Talk to Me and I'll Talk Back" in *Descant*.
"This Man, Just this Once" was a winner in the Short Grain Contest, *Grain*, 1991.
"Getting Back the Nights" in *Snapshots: The New Canadian Fiction*, edited by Kristina Russelo, Black Moss Press.
"Safe Sex" was part of "Tabloid Love, A Dramatic Presentation by the Poets' Combine".
"After 25 Years Still Working it Out" in *200% Cracked Wheat*, Coteau Books, 1991 and in *Snapshots: The New Canadian Fiction*, edited by Kristina Russelo, Black Moss Press.
"When I Take You Home Again" in *Beyond Bad Times*, edited by Vanna Tessier, Snow Apple Press, 1993.
"Watching Me Watching You, Waiting" in *Moosehead Review*.
"Only at Night" in *Scrivener*.
"Did He Dance?" in *Open Windows*, edited by Kent Thompson, Quarry Press, 1988.
"Love Bears the Name" and "Ragnarok" in *Winter of the White Wolf*, NeWest Press, 1989.
"Where Dreams Cannot Rise to Morning" in *Canadian Author*, 1996.
"Setting Out", "Study for *Pas Doleur*", "While the Night Bird Called", and "Woman Locked in the Lussan Clock Tower" in *Prairie Fire*.

This book is dedicated to:
D.L.K. and J.H.
from the time of the Triumvirate: 1984-1994

CONTENTS

FOREWORD   13

I   *AMOUR DE LONGH:* LOVE FROM AFAR

1. *Afternoon Near Riverside*   18
2. *Amour de longh*   25
    THIS MAN, JUST THIS ONCE   28
    MIRROR, MIRROR?   31
    FROM A GREAT DISTANCE   33
    GETTING BACK, THE NIGHTS   35
    STARTING OVER   36

II   UNBORN BABE ALREADY BOUND

3. *Study for Searching for the Nude in the Landscape*   40
4. Setting Out: Notes Towards the Search   42
    LOVE BEARS THE NAME   44
    DID HE DANCE?   46
    LINNAEA, MY TWINFLOWER   47
    AFTER SLEEP:
    DREAMING THE DAY YOUR FATHER LEFT US   49

III   *PAS DOLEUR*

5. *Study for* Pas Doleur   52
6. The Takeover Artist   54

TOO LONG AT THE FAIR	59
TALK TO ME AND I'LL TALK BACK	63
WHEN I TAKE YOU HOME AGAIN, YOU CAN DO ANYTHING YOU WANNA DO, 'CAUSE I DANCED DIRTY WITH YOU	71
WATCHING ME WATCHING YOU, WAITING	73
ONLY AT NIGHT	74
MARIELLA'S WEDDING MARCH	76

IV WHILE THE NIGHT BIRD CALLED

7. *Woman Locked in the Lussan Clock Tower*	84
8. *The Night Bird's Warning*	86
AFTER TWENTY-FIVE YEARS, STILL WORKING IT OUT	89
THE WAY SHE GOES	91
SAFE SEX	93
THE PAST, UNDONE	95
PANSIES	97

V WOMEN DIVING INTO WATER

9. *Women Diving into Water*	100
10. *Farewell to Pont du Gard*	102
MISSING	104
LADYBOAT	105

THE MERMAID IN CHANCE'S POND	107
ONE LOVE SONG CAN ONLY LEAD TO ANOTHER	112
A NIGHT OWL, AN HIBISCUS, A MUD HEN	116
WHILE TREE FROGS SING	117
PENETRATION ROCK	121

VI WHERE DREAMS CANNOT RISE TO MORNING

11. *La Maison Fell*	124
12. *Where Dreams Cannot Rise to Morning*	126
WOMAN FROM SONG	127
CHAINED TO THE RAILING OF THE STEPS THAT LEAD UP TO THE WALL OF HIGH ART	129
THE DRAFT DODGER, THE FLOWER CHILD, THE IBEX	130
WHITE HORSE PEOPLE	132
RAGNAROK	136

VII BEYOND THE *COUILLARDE*

13. *Morning at Pont du Gard*	140
14. *The Night of the Fall*	142
WE HAVE COME TO THIS	145
AFTERWORD	153
BIBLIOGRAPHY	157

searching for the nude in the landscape

— A Catalogue Raisonné —
by
Paul Caron

Contents © Paul Caron, 1996

Compiled and curated by Paul Caron.
Cover design by Paul Caron.
Typesetting and catalogue design by Erica Gunnerson.
Printed and bound in France.

The curator gratefully acknowledges the assistance of the Western Canadian Foundation for the Arts for providing subsistence, travel, research costs, and a retreat house in Lussan to work, in particular to: Gaylene Brockworst for her patient and persistent attention to detail; the Saskatchewan Union of Art Curators for help with crating, shipping, and mounting costs; Dr. David. L. Keening, F.R.C.P, for releasing Christophe Caron's medical files and Estelle Caron's letters and stories; Marcella Pastriami for believing in this retrospective and organizing my first exhibition at the Volti Gallery in Ville Franche Sur La Mer; and finally, Esme Gunnerson Caron (age 4) who saw the underwater sprite and the last eclipse of the moon in her grandmother's final painting before I did.

The publisher gratefully acknowledges the financial assistance of the Western Canadian Foundation for the Arts, the Canadian Arts Research Council, the Department of Literary Heritage, and the City of Saskatoon Arts Trust Board.

Canadian Cataloguing in Publication Data

    Caron, Paul
    searching for the nude in the landscape
    ISBN 1-30658-620-8

1. Artist – Women. I. Title.
        La Terre/Les Mots
        #7 La Rue Reparate
        Nice, France   19 40 54

FOREWORD

My father died before I was born, and my mother spent the rest of her life trying to understand his death and explain him to me.

When I was a child she told me stories at night, long tales that included old family myths passed on by the Gunnerson women, and when we were apart in later years, she wrote me almost daily from whatever exotic port or village offered her temporary refuge. Often, the letter took the form of a story about someone else, and at the time, they seemed to have little to do with me or my mother. Because she believed the emotive power of visual art was evoked through a story it contained, I now believe they were an effort to move beyond the single event (my father's demise) that informed her work towards another artistic phase that never quite materialized on canvas.

And when she died, in 1992, I found most of the paintings of my father contained in this retrospective, together with thousands of studies, sketches, notes. While compiling them, I was struck by something more than what appeared to be an obsessive preoccupation with guilt. Yes, my mother blamed herself for my father's death, and begged me to forgive her. But her search, it seemed to me, was less a failed attempt to move beyond a tragic loss, and more a quest to find herself.

Who was Estelle Caron?

In her lifetime, she was an obscure, relatively unknown artist. And after her passing, I crated and shipped home the work I found in the house in Lussan, then began to show it to curators and critics. While most expressed the importance of a first public exhibition, ironically also a retrospective, it was Marcella Pastriami, Curator of the Volti Gallery in Ville Franche Sur La Mer, who felt the importance of a first viewing in the south of France, so close to Lussan where so much of the work was created. Committed to organizing the exhibit, she asked me to select the work, and prepare a catalogue.

And then began my search.

How does a mother reach beyond her own grief and convey to her son his tragic heritage without transferring her fear as well? How can she interpret for him that intimacy without instilling in him her own passion? One of my mother's greatest fears was that I would end up like my father, and she expressed it in ways that frustrated me in my youth. "You have your father's black eyes," she would say, "but isn't it a blessing they're so mild of expression." When I excelled in mathematics and physical sciences, she channelled my interest towards ancient history, literature, and art history. And though I was given an easel and paint box for my fifth birthday, and thereafter was always encouraged to explore colour, form, patterns, and perspective — even allowed to stay up late if I felt inspired to create — any impulsive act or choice, such as taking up scuba diving, was regarded by my mother as utter foolishness until I arrived at a concrete, well-developed plan of action. "It would be sheer folly to strap a tank to your back and dive into the water," she said. "Go to the library and find out everything about it, and when you know where you will take lessons, from whom, and for how long, then and only then will I invest in the equipment you will need."

The results of my childish research were always greeted with great excitement, and a clapping of paint-stained hands.

Estelle Caron, the mother, gave me the greatest gift a parent can offer a child: the love of learning. Estelle Caron, the artist, believed in what she called "the accident of art", the deeper emotive power contained in the work, unplanned by the artist, that rises to the surface in unexpected moments during its creation and is there waiting to be discovered by someone else. While creating her figures and landscape, she was completely unaware of the hidden artist even I found so difficult to locate, but she is there, in the image of a wood nymph secreted behind heavy foliage, or revealed through the flip of a shirt and a bare foot disappearing behind a stone wall.

For me, the gathering and selection of material to accompany the sketches and finished canvases has been a strange journey, not without frustration when I failed to interpret a painting according to her vision, fraught with pain when my father was finally fully revealed to me.

During my rebellious youth, which was more than a normal attempt to determine one's own identity and destiny, I was afraid I would inherit my father's addiction to mind-altering substances and his obsession with the unobtainable. Twice I ran away, once to my grandmother's Saskatoon home, from whence I was promptly returned by her to my mother, and later, at sixteen, I stole a motorcycle and travelled west, a five day escapade that terrified my mother and ultimately sobered me enough to agree to register for an undergraduate course in Fine Arts the following autumn. I couldn't know it then, but that was a major turning point in my life that, ultimately, led to this search for my mother as artist.

The final selection of work included here was, of course, a subjective one; a less intimately involved critic and curator might have chosen a different "collage" of sketches, notes, paintings, and stories. The focus arrived, quite unexpectedly, when I received dozens of stories and poetry my mother had sent, along with letters, to Dr. David L. Keening, F.R.C.P. of Montreal, my father's analyst who corresponded with my mother for twenty years. (I believe they met twice, once in Saskatoon and once in Montreal.) Though her primary "language" was visual, each and every work she created was based on a narrative, and more often than not Estelle Caron wrote the story or prose poem before she approached the canvas. They certainly provided me with a fascinating adjunct or personal appendix to the major event of her life: my father's demise and its relation to who my mother was before and after that tragic event.

When the analyst repeatedly tried to encourage my mother to write "therapeutic notes" to him — even though she was unwilling to enter into analysis with him or another psychiatrist — Estelle Gunnerson Caron impishly sent him a story instead. When he asked her why she wrote in the third person, she retorted by return mail: *I am always the watcher. I must distance myself from the subject, most especially if that person(a) is me, in order to get an interesting perspective for the viewer or reader. The poet as persona, that self-indulgence is, at best — dull — and doesn't allow me the full range of vantage points required to present a proper scale for the story or its painting.*

Always a trickster, Estelle Caron further turned the analytic tables on the psychiatrist by writing a series of "Charming Dave Stories", a caricature of the Jungian analyst.

There are seven descending levels in the Volti Gallery, and I have, therefore, arranged the exhibit and the catalogue in seven sections. Because I attempted to expand on her search for the exposed self, each level of the former dungeon contains a major canvas, showcases an excerpt from letters she wrote to me and stories she sent to Dr. Keening. On each of the latter, she penned a cryptic note to him. Where possible, I have also indicated when and where in the world she was when she wrote each piece.

Removed now, to what I hope is a proper objectivity by that cathartic search, I offer her legacy to me, together with this catalogue raisonné — our story — as Estelle Caron's gift to the world.

– Paul Caron
Ville Franche Sur La Mer, March 22, 1996

I

AMOUR DE LONGH: LOVE FROM AFAR

*And finally, so afraid of losing
him, I couldn't reach him;
and he, so afraid — or so unwilling —
to find me: lost.*

1. *Afternoon Near Riverside*
c. 1972
37 x 45 cm
Mendel Art Gallery, Saskatoon

The work of Estelle Caron (1952-1992) contained in this retrospective expresses the male's Cézannic fear of women and, therefore, of the violence contained in the physical act of love.

The first, *Afternoon Near Riverside*, a knife-painting, precedes Estelle Caron's erotic prose poems, her graduation from the University of Saskatchewan and her marriage to the francophone engineer, Christophe Emile Caron. Twenty years her senior and a man not known for his capacity for self-irony, he created the facetious title prior to their honeymoon in Provence where the artist, influenced by her discovery of the spirit of Cézanne in Aix-en-Provence, is known to have begun the figure-and-landscape suite, *searching for the nude in the landscape*.

Of unconcealed sexual intensity and heavy mythological allusions, this narrative-painting verges on the pornographic even in the context of the liberating '60s. It foreshadows her stylistic break from the realistic conventions and restrictions that proliferate in prairie landscape art.

Even then, in her earliest phase, her unique combination of figures found within a landscape was viewed from an unusual perspective, this time from above and set at a north-west angle as if the observant artist-as-voyeuse crouched, high, among the heavy arms of a blue spruce. The artist as watcher is a dominant theme, but unlike other master artists, such as Cézanne who painted himself into many landscapes, her presence is strongly felt, rather than seen, as if she is a wood-nymph with magical powers cast over the mortals she directs — with brush and palatte-knife strokes — towards uncontrollable passion.

The heavy laying on of paint with a palatte knife, as if carved and piled by a stone mason, and the swift, shocking, almost frenzied *movement* caused by surprise, are characteristic of Estelle Caron's work.

Here, we follow a wooded path used as a short-cut by caddies between the Riverside Golf Course and the city. Deep in its woody centre we find a tripod and easel, a luminous white easel, blank as a page. Yet, among the deep blue shadows of the tree we find oddly placed the images she would later intensify through enlargement to portray her husband: a cloven hoof, a singular curvaceous haunch, a dark muscular arm with a bird-claw hand, poised, grasping her blue-feathered brush.

Looking down, from an arabesque sweep of branches and leaves reminiscent of the detailed strokes of Ernest Linder's Emma Lake scenes, we find on a serpentine sandy path a scatter of shed clothing: a yellow bandanna, a gypsy skirt, red straw sandals hastily kicked off, a white muslin blouse, and a rope necklace of blue stones. (The necklace is purported to have been given to the artist's mother on her honeymoon at Lake Louise in 1951). In contrast, the male clothing—navy and white—is neatly folded and piled beside brown penny loafers laid precisely beside a plaid car-robe.

Who are the sunbathers broken apart on the picnic blanket?

The notes and letters she wrote to her husband's analyst after his death in 1972 regarding a similar sketch titled *Conceived in the Woods, 1951*, together with the prose poem "Dreams before Birth" that Estelle Caron published in *Descent* in 1982, would indicate that the nude lovers were modelled after her parents. We note the likeness of the woman to the photograph (cat. figure 2) of the artist's mother taken in a rowboat on Lake Louise: the pale freckled skin, her hair the tones and texture of braided sunflower stems, deep brown eyes set close together. But Evelyn Gunnerson's torso was long waisted with no indentation over angular boyish hips, her legs tapering to long narrow feet, with a remarkable big toe twice as long as the others. In sharp contrast, (cat. figure 1) the daughter's face is round with wide-set eyes. She is short, thick waisted, her haunches swell from a swayed back over thighs and lower calves that bunch with tension, even in repose, as if ready to leap up and flee the scene.

Frightened, the young woman has flung herself apart from her lover and landed awkwardly on her right hip against a rock, her head thrown back, her left hand still caught in her lover's mossy chest hair, the right hand and arm cradled around her belly in a protective gesture rather than in an attempt to hide her sex below it. Although naturally plump and chunky legged, the young woman's waist appears thickened in profile, her belly distended but tight. (Estelle Gunnerson was pregnant when she married Christophe Emile Caron.)

In 1972, from Lussan, she wrote to Dr. David L. Keening, her husband's Montreal analyst: *I have always known that my mother's fate and mine will be as entwined as vines in the arbour below Maison Fell.* [Estelle Caron's mother was widowed in 1952, two months before the artist's birth.] *Today I did a Study of a vineyard, searching for the nude, and though I didn't find her, when I was done the charcoal leaves didn't conceal the clusters of male parts, heavy as dark grapes left too long on the vine. I can't yet know what will become of us. Chris is so — distracted and distraught. He stopped taking his pills. Drinks too much Provence wine.*

The lover in the painting bears some resemblance to the artist's father: dark, a humped nose broken too many times on the rugby field. But the eyes — not withstanding the sudden shock of the event — are oval shaped, heavy lidded and red rimmed like Christophe Caron's, rather than round, Nordic blue, unclouded and mild of expression like Gunnerson's in his wedding photo. (cat. figure 3.) Barely longer in torso than the woman's, her lover is darkly hairy about the chest and shoulders, his feet wide and square, the toenails unusually long and raggedly curving. His body jerks upward at an angle, all his weight caught on heavy haunches, arms stretching before him in balance, in an attempt to gain a foothold and grab the intruder. His head is balding, the brow bold, bearing a striking resemblance to her husband's portrait, painted on their honeymoon: shocking up-ended hair, winged eyebrows, the nostrils flared in anger, black pupils blazing with the seemingly sudden change from fear to fury.

While the lovers are contained within the deep shadows of the woods, a hidden Rembrandt light strongly illuminates the intruder at the centre of the canvas, from a perspective and on a scale that would become characteristic of her later work. Crashed to one side of the path, a red CCM bicycle with '50s balloon tires and rusted silver fenders lies among raised sandy dust, its rear wheel blurred with spinning. In the right-hand corner, far below the path, we see a well-groomed golf course, small pin flags, the glint of lifted drivers, sun-visor hats, yellow-trousered golfers. The boy, obviously a caddy, has taken the shortcut from the clubhouse to the city and stumbled upon the nude lovers. In an effort to avoid them, he skidded into the sloping ditch, and fell. In crouched position, one angled leg lifted in takeoff position like a startled grouse, he plunges towards the trees. Though he wears the boat-neck T-shirt of the '50s, white shorts, sneakers and green socks, his hair is hippie length, unevenly cut, straggling and greenish toned like algae in a stony slough.

The most astonishing thing about the young caddy is how much he looks like the older lover: the shock of hair, the dark-rimmed eyes, the flared nostrils. The photograph of Christophe Caron, taken at age 14, in front of his parents' stone house in Longeuil may have served as an inspiration or model for the caddy. (cat. figure 8.)

Like all Caron motifs, there is no ending or closure to what she later called her story-paintings. The teenager may have two choices, the deciding of which will determine his destiny. He may plunge headlong through the forested spruce and poplar and willow, curve his way back to the clubhouse and boastfully rally his friends to hasten back on their careening bikes where he can show them the nudes in the woods. Or, he may stumble home, hot and damp with an unnamed fear, where he will hide in his mother's musty cellar, shivering and consumed, hot-then-cold with first desire. And there, hidden in an old boarded-up coal bin, he will seek release and relief. But obsessed with the unattainable, like Christophe Caron, he will never find it.

Given the artist's complicated worldview and this recurring motif, we may conclude that three stories are collapsed into this painting: her own imagined conception at Lake Louise in 1951, the remembered conception of her son Paul in 1972, and an anecdote written by Caron in a letter to her in 1970 about the first time he saw a nude woman and his longing for the unattainable that he first felt in his mother's basement, which Estelle retold in her 1984 prose poem, "His Mother's Cellar".

Since the artist was raised by a widowed mother who never remarried or, according to her letters to Estelle, ever had another relationship, and given the artist's studies of medieval romances, the *amour courtois* theme of her life and work is not surprising.

Courted and tutored in an antiquated Pygmalion fashion by the older man from afar (Montreal) for nine years before their marriage, it would appear that once the great-love-at-a-great-distance was consummated it was over, a factor which may have contributed more to Christophe Caron's suicide than his then third declaration of bankruptcy.

Born in Marseille, the son of a ship builder, Christophe Caron moved to Montreal with his parents when he was twelve, studied hydraulic engineering at MIT and graduated with distinction. An excessive man, he squandered exorbitant amounts at casinos, bestowed lavish gifts upon people he hardly knew, and had suffered at least two known banishments from established Montreal firms. While it is believed that Estelle married him for financial security as well as an escape from the confines of her domineering and possessive mother, which the artist later described as turning out to be an escape from one dark underwater cavern into another, he apparently kept the truth of his situation from her until the reading of his Last Will and Testament. The failed engineer was destitute.

In his many letters to the artist, Dr. Keening speculated about the hermaphroditic quality of her postmodern muse, its anima-animus theme, the primitive aspect of the hidden artist, Estelle Caron's allegorical self-expression and her husband's extreme sexual preferences.

On June 30, 1982, ten years after her husband's suicide, she wrote to his analyst from Maison Fell in Lussan where they spent their honeymoon: *When we lie between lavender rows or twine together in a Van Gogh field of sunflowers or meld beneath cypress and mulberry and scrub under the massive Pont du Gard it is impossible to know where he begins and I end, such is our union, our fit. When I touch his brow it is mine.* Yet, with a rough-edged scrawl Caron wrote on the back of the last typewritten page:

> *And why, when we are apart*
> *sunning beneath the bridge*
> *or bathing in the River Gardon,*
> *is he unable to see me*
> *his own exposed shadow —*
>
> *a Roman coin*
> *the fossil spine of a fish*
> *the divide and span*
> *the leap across. Transfixed. Yet blind.*
> *Crumble of bone on stone.*

When the analyst wrote back, suggesting she consult him about her inability to get over her loss and stop blaming herself after twenty years and enter a new creative phase she began writing stories — about the doctor. The originals are still in the possession of her family.

2. *Amour de longh*

(Lussan, 1992)

It's so hard to know how much or how little to tell you about your father.

When I met him on a holiday in Montreal with my mother, he looked like the troubadour I still dream of nightly, Jaufre Rudel de Blaye, who first sang of *amour de longh*, love from afar. In front of the flagged Musée de Montreal, he climbed into a tourist carriage on one side, my mother and I on the other side.

Twenty years younger than your father, then only thirteen, I was transfixed by his black, red-rimmed eyes, the flight of his untamable hair. He may as well have worn a troubadour cap, leggings, a diamond-checked doublet.

"Eh, Plumplette," he said. And there began our language game, a combination of English and French.

He was too young for my mother and too old for me.

For nine years, he wrote to me every day, long compositions about his dream of building a causeway to connect Prince Edward Island to the mainland, funding and politics his only barriers.

My provincial education was nothing compared to his lessons on history, art, architecture, and romantic literature. The boys my own age paled into insignificance and I rarely dated, not merely because of my overly strict mother. I was captured by your father's courtly love.

We met only twice before our wedding day, when he came to Saskatchewan, seeking a contract with the provincial and civic governments to design ring roads around the two major cities in our province.

The only constructions he ever completed were asphalt roads.

Yet I was enchanted by a man of great contrasts, of such diverse complexities and wide range of emotions that he soared to great heights, then plunged into ever greater depths. When he was melancholy he never spoke (or wrote) to me, and I know now, twenty years later, that during those blue-black periods he was incapable of action of any kind, even the most mundane chore beyond his grasp. Only when borne aloft by his muse was he able to work or love and then, with such intensity, he couldn't sleep. Such were our few short weeks in Provence.

We went there after our wedding — a civil ceremony since my mother was ashamed that I was pregnant — because your father wanted to show me where Cézanne lived and worked. He insisted I could go beyond the *couillarde* — a coarse word for male virility that Cézanne used for his palette-knife portraits — by finding the female equivalent. And too, your father wanted to return to Pont Du Gard where, he said, his dream of building began as a boy. He believed he could model his causeway on the majestic aqueduct, and he refused to accept that impossibility.

Christophe was all about failed connections, improbable spans, his inability to bridge great gaps in his soul. His personality was bacchic, geometrical, his highs parallel to his lows, with no space for rest between them.

Like an artist, he sought the centre of a creation, but despaired at any flaw. I never knew which way his disappointments would send him: down, into dark caves, or up, to the tops of towers. Watching me sketch or paint, he screamed at me, arms flailing, because I so often couldn't devise the parallel lines, planes, or what he called "the partnership of forms". I only followed the light, then tried to capture on canvas what it showed me. But that wasn't good enough for your father; he wanted more from me.

We couldn't connect or span the bridge between us because my light was parallel to his dark, and he couldn't penetrate it. When I found the light he led me into shadow. When I discovered shadow he pushed me into the sunlight. Leaving my widowed mother's home for Christophe was an escape from one dark underwater cavern into another.

THIS MAN, JUST THIS ONCE

This story wants to begin with rain, its sudden surprise, how it captures the couple. This woman wants it to happen the way it does in the movies: the race for shelter, maybe huddling under an umbrella or his jacket held over their heads. This story wants to take place in an abandoned barn, with the smell of hay, steaming hides, breath caught, a low moan. It wants more of this man than silence, separation.

This man wants a long swift walk along the riverbank — will he hold her hand? — a ten-lap swim in the city pool — will he teach her the crawl or take her on his back? — then seafood, some jazz — will he dance her down? This large long-legged man takes deep strides, frowning, so determined to burn calories. This woman's head barely reaches up to his shoulder, her short legs scissoring to keep up with him. She is comfortable with silence, but too sensitive now to his changing moods, how he curves into himself as the river turns swiftly then rushes under its bridges. If only, just once, it had something to do with her. He carries so much weight: too many nights' work, the need for long-haired women, song. He doesn't even know she cares, worries. Wishes. Under the high hot sun, he changes the course of the river when he sheds his shirt.

This story discards its memories: the old powerhouse falling into the dust of the steep bank, her high school on the other side, her kissing cousin who tipped on his toes under a tree, afraid to touch the innocent night. They didn't come this far. The story abandons the tree-climbing child. The river forgets its history: the Temperance Colony, the Northcôte stuck on a sandbar and tooting its whistle during the last battle, its barges and paddleboats and pirate-ship rafts, even the child drowned and still turning under the dam. There is only this man this woman, just this once.

This story is two thousand years old. It takes note of a half-naked boy on a bicycle, riding in tandem with a sun-drenched girl. He never slows, looks back at her. This man never breaks his stride, or adjusts to this woman's mincing steps. This day she tries but cannot make him laugh when she veils her eyes with her hand and says she's his Hindu woman, or an Arabian wife. He should be her consort and trail ten steps behind her. So she leaps and bounds ahead of him, imitating the way he walks, frowning, squinting, eyes fixed on the footpath. Though he catches up and overtakes her, she remains light, years beyond him. This story can only go in one direction now, end only one way. Under a cluster of new cottonwood a lone man sleeps on his side, one arm flung over his eyes.

This woman and this story have a turning point when they reach the pool. He leans against the riverstone wall, watching the women emerge: hot pink, sun-burnt orange, cool as limes. She perches on a picnic table, easy. If he wants to swim laps, she can lounge on the grass, under a tree. He cannot choose: wait for the water-splashing kids to leave, or fetch the car and head for an indoor pool. The story turns with the changing sky, clouds building high, dark as tarnished silver. It's a long way back to his car.

When the rain begins, he pulls on his shirt. She lifts her face, to catch the rain. Her skin glistens, golden. She swings her arms, she will never tire now. Then under the iron bridge, its girders and high arches rising where pigeons coop, the wind, suddenly as strong as a woman in love hanging sheets on a clothesline, whips her wet hair around her face. She scoots alongside him, slips her left arm through his right one, and hooked at the elbows, their forearms slide together. Wet and sleek as seals. Not cold, the sun still held within her, if only this man, just once, this night.

This story wants to end with rain but closes at a car wash. The sun high again. This woman paces, waiting. She lost the night, first alone in a hot tub, then in the effort of getting out, hiking to his door and yelling, Never again, I'm giving up long rivers, walks with you. Now shaking, this man hoses down his blue Windstar, carefully. Spraying. Water, soft as the night of the rain. He towels it down, beginning at the back bumper, then rubbing the long sleek body, ruffling the chenille, as if drying a beloved horse. Left side. Right side. Circling the hubs, polishing. His body bent, head turned away from her, he's unaware that she is already somewhere else, so far downriver he will have to run to catch her.

◆ ◆ ◆

Dr. Keening:
    You asked me to write about my first memory of Christophe. I don't do therapy. Here's a story, instead. It serves, of course, as notes towards a painting for Paul.

– October 8, 1973
(my birthday)
E.G.C.

MIRROR, MIRROR?

The first time I saw him, I believed he was you. The man halved a breakfast bun exactly the way you do: he curved his left hand around it and pressed on the knife with two fingers, then counted the sugared walnuts, dividing them into two even portions, one for the person across the table I couldn't see for the palm frond and the other for himself; that man had your fine-boned fingers, and he talked with them the way you do too. He looked at me out of your slanted green eyes. I didn't interrupt what I thought was a client meeting, and hastened to the lobby, then down the stairs to the conference room where I found you at a table, holding a place for me and half of your cinnamon bun.

The second time, I was missing you in another city, counting the nights until I would see you again. Driving to Safeway to replace the candles we burned at both ends the nights we couldn't sleep on the road, we almost hit head on, your twin and I. The white car cutting around in front of me was yours. The man driving it had your arched brow, its deep furrows, your brown hair swept back and curling up from the collar of your leather jacket. He looked at me out of your green eyes. I was afraid I would see myself navigating in the bucket seat beside him, unable to tell which cars were moving away or approaching, no connection between dots on the map, divided by words, yet connecting, your impossible profile caught in the sideview mirror.

There is a third and last time for everything. A weather watch at the window, I waited for you. Your car curving around the crescent. And there he was, on the other side of the street, striding the way you do, feet splayed out, his weight heavier on the left leg, the opposite of how you lean to the right, head swinging. Your leather jacket, hands thrust deep into the pockets. He turned left as you turned right. Another split second and you would have hit him head on.

And now, out of place in yet another city, I light a candle and leave it in your shadow.

If you want nothing, need nothing of me, he will come to me, your double.

♦♦♦

Dr. Keening:
    I'm into double images now, Christophe's and mine. Don't ask me what it means. I'm just the artist. Look up the old myths, if you like, but they won't tell you why or how we were split in two.

– October 10, 1973
Regina
E.G.C.

FROM A GREAT DISTANCE

It was the darkest night of her year.

Beyond the castle hotel, a straw-hatted horse hauled a surrey up the bridge, with two motorcycles at her flanks.

The fast-flowing river water lay thick and flat around sandbars as if seeking respite before it dashed under five bridges. It resisted the pull of the moon's light. On the riverbank, old flattened grass waited for new green shoots, that replacement. The wind, high and cold and piercing, swept gritty sand into piles on the edges of the paved path.

His coattails flapped about his knees. She huddled under her Aquascutum.

At the top of the bridge, traffic lights changed: green to amber to red. Only the red light cast down upon the dark water. When the lights changed the green was invisible, the water caught no reflection at all. Dockside, they leaned on the railing, elbows touching. Shivering, they stared at the black water, at street lights shimmering on its surface.

The university hospital across the river looked like a prison, a castle, and a spaceship, so many wings and bridges had been added to the original riverstone structure by so many different architects and stonemasons.

She saw a gondola then, the cables connecting the riverbanks. It carried some of her professors from their homes on this side of the river to their classrooms and cubbyholes. She wanted to abandon her studies and leave with him when he returned to Montreal.

He said, No, not until you graduate. He tilted the teeter-totter, held the saddle on the ground with one heavy foot, then let it down. Easy.

The islands bared to the wind, the low waterline, their isolation, and an empty rowboat buffeted by waves and bumping against the bank made her feel the seductive pull of the dark water.

Lurking there, in the shadows of a gazebo, a wild-haired, wild-eyed man curled around his flask, protecting it.

She gazed at the castle hotel, its gardens dark and dead.

He took her hand then, pulled her away from the water, up the stone steps, across the gritty street to her mother's apartment door.

After he had gone, she opened the glass doors onto the balcony, let the gusting wind into her room, then stepped out, trying to guess which room in the castle hotel was his.

It started to rain.

In front of the castle hotel, wind toyed with the fringes on the surrey, the straw-hatted horse lay down on her side, her belly heaved, and the top-hatted driver thrust his cold hands deep in his pockets.

♦♦♦

D.L.K.:
I revisited the riverbank today, then wrote this for my son Paul. Tomorrow I will return, begin a sketch: Dockside. Don't fish off the company dock, sir.

– October 8, 1973
Saskatoon
E.G.C.

GETTING BACK, THE NIGHTS

She says she's found a way to get back the nights we didn't make love. She means to take them all back, the nights she says I bolted from her, left her to burrow alone in bed, no comfort in the leftover Blue Nun. Get back at me, more like it. I'm supposed to take my shower then see the surprise she's got for me. In the driveway. So I'm nervous as a half-fucked fox and just as naked when I look out and see she's taken the rear window right out of the car. And I'm flying out, flapping my arms and yelling about breaking and entering, the trunk's hood rattles on its side on the lawn, and the backseat too. Well, blow me down gently, she's made a big soft bed in the back, her French comforter and feathery pillows all puffed up, and she's cozy as can be, cooing too. She says she's put it right and we're going back, and I don't know how she does it but the car starts rolling backwards, and she's got me diving in, right through the open back window. She's got it in her kind of cruise control. Backwards. Going back to all the northern nights, lights dancing above the river. The bridge of stars is aligned now, she says. She's set the course and doesn't stop till we're back, in the Saskatchewan valley of our beginning nine years ago. It's a celebration, she says. She's taken me back to all the unrequited nights. The rest is up to me.

❖❖❖

Doctor Keening:
    So I tried to put my self in his shoes, tried to hear him again, put it right. Failed once more. Maybe it's my answer to the *Couillarde*?

– Estelle
May 21, 1973
Saskatoon

STARTING OVER

She was always starting over. Trying again. Harder.

She didn't know exactly when she stopped doing that, and if her son asked her she wouldn't tell him it was after her husband had destroyed her pansy bed, not only because he wouldn't understand — what have flower beds got to do with anything?

Her design was clear and simple.

At the greenhouse, she wandered between rows, the hothouse steam rising, the light slanting through glass panes. She kicked off her sandals and wiggled her toes in the muddy path. She held a chrysanthemum in both hands, burrowed her nose in global peony heads. Rubbed dark earth between her fingertips.

She knew exactly what she wanted now.

Only perennials survived winter.

At home, after working peat moss into freshly turned soil, she lay out the plants, arranged them just so, then dug five holes. The spade felt hard under her foot, the wooden handle rough in her hands. Then she lifted the pyramid junipers and set them into the holes at each end of the flowerbed. She shovelled in rich dark earth, packed it down. Between the junipers she planted three dwarf evergreens. Then she stretched, rubbed the small of her back. Kneeling, she planted Oriental poppies, peonies, long-stemmed daisies, tiger lilies. Wet earth formed giant scabs on her bare knees, but she dug her toes into the soil, packing, smoothing earth, spraying.

When she was finished she sat on the front step until nightfall, breathing in the new scent. Just before the streetlights blinked on, she rose, stiff and sore, but satisfied.

She climbed into her car, turned the key, and left.
She was starting over.
Once, she looked back, at the flowerbed.
The everlasting flowers.

◆◆◆

D.L.K.:
>If this doesn't tell you about my new beginning for Paul, you aren't half the shrink you think you are; and I'm not leaving town.

E.
– May 24, 1973
(Likely Regina. P.C.)

II

UNBORN BABE ALREADY BOUND

*The story-painting comes from me
but it is not me. Just like you.
I can imagine your eyes. Perhaps
they will be as black as your father's
but as mild of expression as my father's,
with an oval slant like mine. They can only be
your distinctive eyes because of what you will see
and how you will react to that vision.*

3. *Study for searching for the nude in the landscape*
   c. 1972
   Pencil, charcoal, green and blue chalk
   23.6 x 17.2 cm
   Private Collection

One of the freest of the Provence studies, and typically soft and tonal like the later prairie portraits, this drawing is believed to have been sketched towards dawn on the seafront balcony of the Beaulieu hotel where the Carons stayed on June 26, 1972 before setting out for Aix-en-Provence.

It holds a bold allusion to Cézanne's *Contrastes*, painted in 1870 and originally part of the decoration of the salon of the Jas de Bouffan. While Cézanne's *portrait-a-deux* of a bearded man and the profile of his younger lover immerses the lovers in an unnamed sea below the prow of a boat, Caron's sketch, painted from the left side of the balcony (artist concealed except for a pale bare foot with toes curled on the rung of the railing), directs the eye from an empty bed with love-tossed pillows and tangled shroud-like sheets in the lower left corner, upward, through opened French doors, to the waterfront.

From the top right corner a convertible Fiat races out of the Monaco tunnel. The typical Caronian hidden light, this time the incandescent blue that drew artists like Picasso, Pissarro, Duffy, Van Gogh, Monet and Matisse to the Côte d'Azure, reveals the heads and shoulders of departing lovers immersed and floating in a shimmering water-like sky. The artist depicts Christophe Caron with weedy tendrils snaking away from a bold brow, his black eyes sunken. The hair of the woman beside him, in profile, trails prophetic black mourning ribbons, the mouth set with resignation. Foamy clouds breathe around their bare shoulders, clothe the curving elliptical shapes of their bodies.

On the rumpled pillow, where two heads have left their impression, lie a blue breast feather and a green claw.

4. Setting Out: Notes Towards the Search
   (Lussan, June 27, 1972)

If you are a boy I will call you Paul, if a girl, then Pauline.
Tonight, after I felt your first flutter-kick or elbow nudge, I rose, driven to record for you your parents' search, mine for the nude in the landscape, your father's for the dream of a great builder of bridges. This urgency is born of something I don't understand and therefore can't explain, why I am compelled to save for you the story of our married days together, to give you a preserved memory of your father.
At first, I thought the feeling of déjà vu was caused by your kick against my soft interior walls, or the thunderous bass of a car radio echoing from the mountain tunnel out of Monaco. Lying beside your still-sleeping father, I imagined the music came from a red Fiat, driven by some casino-crazed playboy and a sun-bronzed blonde who would drive all night into a hazy, stone-strewn oblivion. As its booming beat faded, it was replaced by a sing-song wail on the waterfront below, so low and raspy I couldn't tell if it came from a bereft sailor or street-walker. The shatter of glass on cement. Then I heard one double-word yelled — was it in English? — *Visa-cunt!*
Prickling with guilt, having forsaken my freedom for your father's affluence and need to support you at a time when single parenting is still a long way from acceptance in our provincial city, I sensed an approaching *touch*, promising an emergence, an opening as if a metal door into a mountain were about to swing wide and reveal to me an inner truth — the dark side of light,

perhaps. And that revelation, as old as allegories, folktales, myths and magic, could only come to me where midnight black can change to grey to blue to azure.

The *touch* was real. Your father's fingers brushed my shoulder. It stilled me with anticipation, though I hadn't moved even in response to your strong kick.

He didn't sleep on the flight over, though he lay prone in the deep seat, a night mask over his eyes as if he were going to New Orleans or Uzès at Easter. He didn't speak, not once in six hours, and breathed heavily beside me while I read about then dreamed of the Provencal troubadour, Jaufre Rudel de Blaye who first sang of the *amour de longh*, love from afar. He looked like your father in a harlequin costume.

Now, he tapped my shoulder, then opened his mouth, and pointed to a gold-capped molar, groaning.

"I thought you were going to tell me something important," I said.

He said, "If a person has an abscess and doesn't have a root canal for five weeks could he — perhaps die — of say — blood poisoning?" His exhaled breath reminded me of slough water, rank root-rot, decaying vegetation.

"We'll find a dentist as soon as we arrive in Aix," I said. "If it doesn't hurt I wouldn't worry, the nerve is probably dead."

"*Pas douleur*," he said.

LOVE BEARS THE NAME

I am the child lifted
onto my father's heaving chest.
His raven hair sweeps back
into wings.
What's going to happen
to my holy-hecker?
his last words, beating
through walls turning.
A dark-hooded woman
leads me to another room
where stained glass
refuses the morning.

A box lined with satin
will hold his sleep.
I believed I took away

> *his last long breath.*
> *He has gone to the War.*
> *He floats under ice.*
> *He has gone to Winnipeg.*
> *I will find him if I reach*
> *for the red sky.*

I dream of the men who took my father away
on a bed with straps, away in a wailing car.
Into my hands my mother thrusts
a small red box. A snake
writhes around her fingers. Inside the box
her wedding ring sinks into leaves soft as dust.

*On a sleigh-shaped bed
my mother slides over ice.
She screams herself awake
from an endless fall.
Morning is the hardest.
Basement cold. Night ashes
in the furnace. No coal.
She struggles to her school,
falls on ice. And stars
stare down: red.*

*She tells me my father's dream:
when his father died
he found him boarding a plane.
He couldn't stop his father
from flying away.*

*Love bears the name of our fathers,
of their leaving
themselves
behind.*

❖❖❖

– January 12, 1979
My mother's 70th birthday.
Saskatoon
E.G.C.

DID HE DANCE?

Dorothy told me they buried my father under the ice. She was four whole years older. She took me to her church after supper. The girl with brilliant hair twirled, flimsy skirt flared. She's going straight to hell, Dorothy said. The girl's red mouth opened: she howled. She fell down, and her hair hid her face. See? Dorothy said. She gripped my hand. The screen went dark, the lights came on, and Dorothy led me down the rows of bowed heads to the back of the hall. A woman in a blue dress made me kneel on the seat of a chair. The scabs on my knees hurt. Her father died, Dorothy said. They put him in a box lined with satin and buried him under the ice. Was he baptized or christened? the woman said. That means was he dunked or sprinkled, Dorothy said. The woman said, Did he drink? Did he smoke? Did he dance? Pray for your father's soul! On the way home, crossing the skating rink, I twirled circles on the ice. I fell down. I brushed away the snow. The ice was clear and blue. I pressed my face into thin snow, tried to see my father buried there, his last pale unshaven face, his last dance.

❖❖❖

Dr. David:
    Yes, Christophe was twenty years older. I never saw him as a father. Don't go Freudian on me. Here there can be no memories of a man who died before I was born, only a shadow. Under ice.

Estelle.
– January 21, 1979
Saskatoon

LINNAEA, MY TWINFLOWER

Nothing could ever separate them. With her head on his shoulder, his right arm loosely around her, she believed nothing — and no one — could ever come between them. She looked up at him, studied that perfect oval face, the round slope of his cheek curving down to the right angled jaw. With fingertip traced the wide arc of his lips. She tilted the tip of his nose up and he turned his head away from hers. In profile, the end of his nose pointed, his chin, he looked like a different man: thinner. The underfed look was what had made her want to take him home and feed him, no end to that. No end to the struggle, to the control she gave him and her fight to take it back. The separation and the division of goods, two of everything, came when he least expected it. They would never be the same again.

No one could tell the twins apart. On the ultrasound screen, they looked like evergreen twinflowers, with long woody-stem legs, bell-shaped petal heads. Inseparable, even when that single egg divided in two and twinned its identical cells into even halves. Their hands were joined, one left one right, round intertwined leaves, and they were lifted from their mother with hands still clenched. They were twinflowers, with her dark hair and wide eyes, his large sensual mouth and cameo nose. The grandparents marvelled at the perfect combination, called them the monkeys, See and Do. No end to the tricks, the trouble doubled. Only the parents could tell them apart, though they said they didn't know how they did it. The firstborn exactly like her easygoing father, careful to watch both ways when crossing the street, led her sister by the hand. She was swifter with sums and dividing two groups of two. The secondborn exactly like her mother, at the top of the waterslide, dared her sister to go first;

she was quick to leap then look behind her. She was faster with words, but wanting to make the story better, she rubbed out too hard, with eraser shredded the paper, then tore it into two pieces. After the parents split.

After the story, she lies between them, with her head on her firstborn's shoulder, the second child asleep, left arm slung loosely across her stomach. She looks up at the daughter most like the father, that full face changed in profile, high brow furrowed now. His right angled jaw, the chin jutting, and in the slant of the child's blue-green eyes, she sees him.

She calls to tell him how she knows them apart.

◆ ◆ ◆

> For Cousin Lin Gunnerson Albright
> Christmas, 1980
> From Provence.

AFTER SLEEP:
DREAMING THE DAY YOUR FATHER LEFT US

On the day your father left us, the people in white came to the blue hills and changed everything forever. I had bought a white rabbit for you. On the wide lawn that sloped down to the river, shading our eyes against the glare of whirring blades, the white-hot sun and the artificial wind, your father and I watched helicopters land on the banks. People in white jumped down and greeted us by scratching our left arms. They told us we would fall asleep, unable to dream, and when we awoke we would have no worries and — no memories. I turned to your father, but he was gone from my side. I started up the stairs, the drug bringing me to my knees, closing my eyes, but I crawled, up, protecting the newborn rabbit. Your father once told me that ascension in dreams means the attainment of knowledge, but I was not asleep. When I reached the top, it felt like hours later, and I was able to stand, open my eyes. The door to your father's room had been left open, he was bare on the bed that rocked like a cradle from side to side, his back to me, and all I could see of his new woman was one long leg thrust between his knees, her white-blonde hair spilling on the pillow. Their clothes hung on the door of a free-standing cupboard. I fled into the front bedroom with the white rabbit, and stood before the window, waiting for you. I clung to the memory of your father, your grandparents. Once, I looked back, through slats in a window set in the wall between rooms, and saw them deep in the after-sleep, her head on his shoulder, their legs entwined. When they emerge from that room they will not know you, me, but he is your father and I am your mother who loved you before the takeover. And after the woman, her people in white.

❖❖❖

David:
    Is it possible to dream while awake? I wrote this for Paul. When he's older. It was a kitten, but I made it a rabbit, for you.

Estelle.
Happy New Year, 1981, from Provence.

III

PAS DOULEUR

*It was his eyes — so intense — that transfixed me.
I was captured by a man of great contrasts,
of such diverse complexities and wide range of emotions
he soared to great heights then plunged to even greater
depths. Impossible spans.*

5. *Study for* Pas Douleur
c.1972
Pencil, pastels
10.2 x 13.4 cm
Private Collection, Aix-en-Provence

Exceptionally close to the oil on canvas of the same title, this Study rehearses variations of the *nude in the landscape* motif. Although the Caronian perspective rings true — this time the artist, seated on a stone bench, head bent and straw-like tresses falling over a sketchbook, views the scene from the right — the viewpoint is akin to Daumier, copied by Cézanne, who caricatured the prevalence of Venus as a subject for painters in the Salon.

In the foreground, rows of lavender roll towards the subjects like a parade of flower-covered coffins laid end to end. Dentist and patient are illuminated by light filtering through oddly arranged sombre cypress trees. The dentist's chair is engulfed by Van Gogh sunflower stalks, with yellow heads turned bashfully away from the nude dentist. He is a caricature of Picasso: bald and bull-headed. Sunflower stalks coil around his legs and torso, their heads replacing his ears. Body in profile, syringe raised and parallel to an oversized erection emerging from grape leaves, the dentist has swung his head towards the artist and grins at her lewdly.

The focal point, of course, is the patient, who lies with legs pinched together on the couch, lips clamped tight within a heavy Cézanne beard, eyes rolling upward but not yet able to see the nude languishing in a cave cut deep into close-set cypress above his head. Reclining on one hip, garlands woven into her pale hair, Venus leans as if from a boudoir bed, offering a yellow rose, its promise of ultimate farewell, to the patient. The subject's penis, done later with fine brush-strokes, is part of the trunk of a grapevine, the testicles a cluster of green grapes bunched beneath surrounding leaves. It bears an allusion to the phallus engraved on Pont Du Gard called The Hare or The Gopher.

6. The Takeover Artist

(Lussan, June 28, 1972)

After we checked into Hotel Paul Cézanne near La Gare in Aix, I found a dentist on the first floor of a Victorian building that needed sand-blasting, new shutters, paint. We crept down a dark corridor, peeked through an open door, and your papa startled the dentist who looked like Picasso: bald and bullish. I swear he locked the double doors behind us. Your papa lay down on the couch, pointed to his jaw — and turned yellow.

It was only an ulcer, but the dentist said it could go on a voyage, popping up all over your papa's face as well as inside his mouth. For 115F we got a prescription for mouthwash. And the dentist told me not to let your father eat strawberries.

While watching the dentist clean the ulcerated gum, I imagined them both nude.

I didn't know until that moment that the muse could be male or of the narcotic effect the imagination can have on fear and pain.

And then, for the first time, I moved the landscape indoors.

Cézanne said that nothing painted in the studio could ever equal what was done outdoors: the contrast of figures with open air settings. Your father wanted me to copy him, but I resisted, compelled to follow the light where it led me. Even before our honeymoon I had been loathe to make love inside and lured your father out of the car behind barns, down to the riverbank, or into my mother's sunflower garden at home. Here, it was harder to find privacy. So I isolated the patient, surrounding him — and the dentist — by what the light carried into the room from the window.

After the visit to the dentist, my search for the nude muse began in earnest; I was driven, once I fully realized that time and place could dissolve in a painting, people superimpose upon each other, and that, dreamed or imagined, Cézanne's *plein-airisme* contained its equal and opposite reversal. Rather than contrast figures and landscape, the land and its meanings may be brought *inside* as a way of showing how we come from and are part of the earth and that all it holds and promises is in us too. In either setting, the mindscape may be tapped and revealed. The final painting must be an orgy of colour!

But even now, trying to put it into words for the first time — for you — I feel a loss of faith, of integrity, of ownership. The story and its painting comes from me, you see, but is not me. Just like you. I can imagine your eyes. Perhaps they will be as black as your father's but as mild of expression as my father's, with an oval slant like mine; yet they can only be your distinctive eyes because of what you will see and how you will react to that vision.

When I showed him my sketch, your father laughed, the only time he was amused in France, and I gave in and fed him strawberries and cream in the bath that night.

Then we had our first fight.

He wanted me to give a name, not so much to the sketch, but to the technique I explored. I resisted: who was I to be so presumptuous to think I might create something new. "I don't like labels," I said. "You either believe when you see it or you don't. Either way, I made you laugh, and that's what's most important to me: how you feel when you look at it."

He flung his arms up, knocking the bowl of strawberries from my hand and dashing the spoon to the floor. "You must do it," he said, "so the world will understand. And the critics won't mess with it and get it all wrong."

Picking strawberries from my lap and dropping them into his bath water, I said, "It can't be explained. It's just there, that's the way I see it, and if you see something else in it that's good too."

"What what what? What do you see? It has to have a name, not what you did in that dentist's office, what you did to him and to me, but HOW YOU DID IT!" He smacked the surface of the water with both palms, and red berries bounced and bobbed and ducked like mischievous goblins, evasive watersprites.

"I didn't do anything. I just saw a movement, a placement of things, and then I changed them around and brought the land to the people in that room. It's not so difficult. It was — just fun." With a towel, I mopped the spilled cream, the scummy water sloshing over the rim of the tub. Slowly, I crawled backwards.

While he jumped up, shouted, "Girder, cantilever, suspension," slapping the tiled wall, "bascule, jack-knife, pontoon," yanking on the towel rack, "and book-end bridge!" With both fists he hammered the underside of the soap shelf so hard the brackets popped their bolts, bottles and brushes and jars jumped and toppled over the edge; and it all crashed into the tub. Then, arms flailing and wet hair flapping about his soggy shoulders, Chris flew into a frenzy, jumping out of the tub, his bare feet crunching on shales and points of glass, till he was slipping in blood and soap-slime, raving: "Fun? Fun! Do you think the men riding the steel beams swung up to the highest arch or the riveters running far out over the water to the end of the span are having FUN?"

Crouched against the wall, I said, "Chris, your feet, you're bleeding, stop this."

"You've got to understand the partnership of forms if you're going to create — anything — an aqueduct or a painting that will span the ages. You must know how many tons of steel will hold aloft two railway tracks so a train can pass at ninety miles per hour or how many pounds per square foot weight is borne by the most violent wind or how much stress one half hour of sunlight adds to a girder. And, you absolutely MUST know the difference between balancing piers, scaffolding, brackets, and a goddamn pontoon. And to do that you must be able to NAME!"

"So there," I said, feeling your second kick, high, just under my breastbone. I patted what I believed to be an overly-long big toe, just like my mother's. I strangely felt more grief than fear at the beginning of loss. It was the first time your presence brought me solace.

He crashed against the ancient door, it banged shut, and he slid down against it, like a child throwing a tantrum is stopped by some object outside himself suddenly hurtling out of control, and it scares him. He stared at his bloody feet.

I threw a towel at him. "I'm not giving in," I said. "Even your child knows better. And nudged me to prove it."

He said, "It's just because I believe so thoroughly — in your — extraordinary — gift. That I know you — must name define challenge and rename — all the forms."

Melting, your father was all soapy scum and steam and sweat and yes, tears. While I picked bits of glass from his toes and applied ointment and band-aids, he felt your presence for the first time, cradling what we both imagined was your heel in his calloused palm.

You kicked again, and your father said, "He will be a shipbuilder like my father."

❖❖❖

In this letter to her unborn son, four lines are crossed out heavily at the bottom of the page. In light of Estelle Caron's poem, "Unborn Babe Already Bound", in which a mother hopes her child will be a girl, "with unfettered cornflower hair/ yet already bound at the helm of a ship riding low in the sea/ with its heavy load of grain/ bound for Africa" we can assume the artist's response to the father's assumption of gender was a sharp retort.

The fierce sexual tension and struggle for control between the brooding obsessive engineer and the compulsive artist are reflected in later notes when she called him *"My Takeover Artist"*. *"It led us,"* she wrote to me in 1992, *"to the violence and tragedy that occurred at Pont du Gard five weeks later."*

— P.C.

TOO LONG AT THE FAIR

He's been away too long, Charming Dave, the talking shrink.

She talks to him anyway.

She's mute, but she talks to him. If Charming Dave won't return her call, what else can she do? When she says she's not interested in his pathology — who gave him those black Irish eyes? — she's lying.

No one else can see him.

He understands so well now what she says with her hands, her green eyes, the way her body moves down the alley towards the hospital.

She leads her cow with no tail by a rope, and the child with one toe missing on her left foot rides its swaying back.

She takes her cow and the child everywhere.

No one else can see them.

After four days at the Sally Ann she has to move her cow on, that's the Army rule.

She bangs her shopping bag against a trash can. The cow wants to poke its nose in the can, smelling fodder no doubt. She yanks the rope, and the child on the cow's back kicks with her good foot.

On the hospital stairs she stops, tugs at her cinch belt, fixing it over the tops of her flared skirt and full slips. It's chilly, and she's wearing all her ruffled petticoats today. She tucks her straying white hair under her gypsy scarf, checks her lips and lashes in her compact mirror for smears, then marches the cow up the steps and through the doors into Charming Dave's ancestral home.

She treads softly on old oak, strokes the dark bannister leading up to the gallery of tricksters in oils — not hospital honchos — to her they're all Davids with black Irish eyes. They all smile on one side of their faces. Charming Dave winks at her. The cow moos. It leaves pies on the tiled floor. The child cries, her missing toe hurts. The mute woman fingers the frame around his great-uncle and says to Dave, You have a naughty gene. You should isolate it, incubate it, inoculate it before it's too late.

And unlike Henry Higgins or even himself then, he don't talk at all, just shows her. A wild rose in his lapel and a silver helmet on his head, he takes up his fife and drum, no musket needed this time because she's willing to sign the hospital's guest register. And while he plays she sways, her small feet sliding, inverted heels turning in her running shoes. Her ancestors conquered his in the 10th century and left, in the 12th, names like Dolittle, but this is here and now. She shakes her ruffled petticoats at him, swirls her skirt, arms and hands signing a language older than new world snow. She's forgotten the words, lost in a dance older than rain. She dances, dances out her story for him.

They left her, Dolittle Dottie, to mind the cow with no tail. They left her and went to the Fair, her Mamma and Papa, both brothers. She milked the cow in the morning, fed it sweet clover at night, picked stones from its hooves at noon. But they never came back from the Fair, oh never came back at all. They said if she minded the cow, oh, they'd bring her a ribbon or two, bangles and bows and a scarf for her hair, candied apples and floss from the Fair. But they never came back, no they never returned when the car hit a tanker of oil. Oh, the cow with no tail gave no milk at all, and it trod on her toe, her left little toe when they didn't come back from the Fair. The toe turned black, the toe turned green, the toe soured and rotted and smelled. It fell right off and she didn't yell she didn't scream, didn't even cry when they stayed too long at the Fair.

She loses the rhythm, her rhyme. She can't dance a jig, can't shuffle hop step, fulap fulap, doesn't know how to stomp and tromp, and her arms won't stiffen and hold tight to her sides. She stops dancing and bows. Charming Dave applauds.

She'll settle for a cozy chat with him. She wants to show him the tail of ribbons she braided for her cow, the rainbow on his ceiling.

She's dying to know what happens next.

His secretary talks in turns to her and to Charming Dave on the phone. Her name is Olga. She holds her hand over the mouthpiece. She shouts at the mute bagwoman: "HE'S AT A CONFERENCE ON HOMELESS STREET PERSONS." She can't see Charming Dave kissing better the child's toe. She can't see the cow stamping its hind feet. It needs a new tail for swatting flies but it isn't very interested in kissing better. Olga yells, "COME BACK IN TWO WEEKS. I CAN GIVE YOU AN APPOINTMENT THEN."

"I'm mute, not deaf," Dorothy says. She clamps her hand over her mouth. The child counts her toes and asks what number comes after four.

Where is Charming Dave?

On the telephone. Talking to Olga. Checking in, is he?

Olga makes secret signs, pointing at the telephone, then down the hall. She says Dave wants her to go to Emergency. The resident doctor will admit her to the Holding Unit.

"But I want Dave," Dorothy says. She just might give him what he wants: tears for the toe, for the cow's tail.

Olga holds out the telephone, an offering. "Talk to him. He'll talk back."

The cow chews its cud. The child rocks, anxious to be off.

And Dorothy cradles the receiver against her ear. "How are things in Glocca Morra?" she says.

His answer so soft, so far away she barely hears him say:

Bring Dottie to the Fair.

"Meet me in Saint Louis, Louis?"

Yes, meet me at the Fair.

♦♦♦

David:

    Sorry I missed you. I found this story in your office. Don't you love Dottie? And Olga was great. I'll write a proper letter when I get to Lussan.

—June 30, 1991
Nice Airport

TALK TO ME AND I'LL TALK BACK

It isn't true Charming Dave went to Harvard so he could return to Moose Jaw and cure Dirty Daphne though Daphne still believes one day he will discover why she was born with no colour to her skin her hair her eyes and find a way to restore that pigment. But she doesn't want to be cured of all the crazy things she does, why spoil all the fun and anyway, what would the Lutheran Ladies' Aid, the IODE and the Women's Temperance League talk about if Dirty Daphne's house were closed down by the city fathers? Never mind the city mothers.

She dreams constantly of Dave's return.

And he long ago forgot about Dirty Daphne, how for two red licorice and a classic comic Daphne would drop her drawers and show the guys her pink bum, usually hanging upside down from the branch of the cottonwood in her mamma's backyard. Sometimes she fooled around in the tool shed.

The classic comics were always for Davey who waited at the bottom of the garden beside the raspberry bushes, hoping this time she'd get *Tale of Two Cities* or *Robin Hood*. He held onto her coke bottle glasses so they wouldn't get broken. And after the guys hooted and hollered for Daphne's mamma to come out, and after she did invite them in and they lost their nerve instead of their virginity and took off, Davey and Daphne ate the red licorice and traded comics, always in the shade of the cottonwood because Daphne's skin burned so easily and the bright sunlight hurt her weak eyes. Even then, a boy who always got *talkative* on his report card, Dave would always say to Daphne, "Why do you do that?"

"What's it to you?" Daphne said. And Dave climbed the fence into his own backyard, though Daphne always believed he had told her she looked like Shirley Temple with all those curls and she'd grow up to look like Jean Harlow.

The truth is: he was thinking, *Maybe Marilyn Monroe.*

The truth is: once Charming Dave met the willowy and willing Boston Barbara, a nurse of course, and he was so charming and she was so charmed, he really just forgot all about his promise to Daphne.

He forgot his last night in Moose Jaw.

He forgot how the Moose Jaw Dreamboats were rockin' an' rollin' at Temple Gardens, how he glued himself to the stagline wall, not knowing what a good jiver he was and how the girls hoped he would ask them to dance. Charm came naturally to Charming Davey but he didn't always know he had it. He palmed the sides of his Brylcreamed bogie cut, combed and fluffed up his cream puff, and rolled his shoulders under his white sports coat, hoping he looked cool instead of nervous. Then he saw Daphne, sitting alone on the stage steps, heard the guys snickering about pink eyes and white snatches. He saw Daphne scramble to her feet and dash outside, though Daphne remembers he and he alone asked her to dance, a slow waltz, and he gave her his pink carnation when he said goodbye and promised to come back to her with a cure.

Oh yes, Charming Dave has forgotten how the sax wailed "Blue Moon" into the warm night, how he found Daphne in the parking lot, swaying and sobbing and holding herself, her hair pale as the moon, and how the guys were chug-a-lugging a scoffed beer. He's forgotten how they made a beeline for Daphne, chains on their draped pants clanking, coins jingling in their pockets. No red licorice.

But Daphne, sipping gin and lemonade on her porch swing and waiting for Charming Dave, remembers in the hot summer nights when her residents have taken their sleeping pills and she's alone to dream, oh how well she remembers Dave suddenly there, one arm around her cinch-belted waist, saying, "She's my girl. Bug off."

And then he walked her home, there *was* a blue moon, she borrowed his comb, but all he did was kiss her forehead when he said goodbye.

He was the only boy who just wanted to talk.

And now, too many years later, Charming Dave has been asked by his own mum in Moose Jaw and the Department of Health and the City Council, in that order, to intervene and settle the dispute between Dirty Daphne and the lobbying blue-haired ladies.

"Dirty Daphne keeps a clean house, " the mayor said.

She operates an unapproved boarding home for psychiatric patients.

"Her social programs and her recreational activities are getting her in trouble," Dave's mother said.

"It all runs in her family," they all said.

For three generations, women with white gloves and flowery hats have tried to close down Dirty Daphne's to no avail.

"How can we expect Dave to succeed?" the Mayor said.

"No one else can charm like Davey," his mamma said.

Moose Jaw was never the best place to start up a Bed and Breakfast. Daphne's great-grandma was ousted by the redcoats in the rum-running days, and her grandma re-established the business when Moose Jaw was known as Little Chicago during prohibition. Then Daphne's mamma took over and continued to operate the best house north of the 49th parallel and east of the Rocky Mountains. She said Daphne's father was a switchman, a Soo lineman, but she couldn't be sure which one.

After the night of the blue moon, Daphne was determined to get respectability and she soon turned Dirty Daphne's into a boarding home.

The trouble was — and is — cooking three meals a day, washing and ironing welfare clothes, supervising medications and naps, is just so *boring*. So Daphne and her residents play dress-up, using the wigs and hats and gowns in the attic trunks. They play parade. They party. Of course Daphne teaches them how to jive to all the old records. On Tuesdays they wear '50s bathing suits and go swimming at the YMCA. On Thursdays the men wear charcoal suits and pink shirts, the women wear bobby sox and saddle shoes, and they go bowling. On Saturday nights they hit the Harwood Hotel bar in strapless gowns and white sports coats. And at the end of the month when the welfare cheques arrive they throw a big party. Just like in the old days. Sometimes the boys from the CPR or the airbase show up and Daphne does some pretty heavy making out, you betcha. It starts with a broom dance, progresses to a snake dance down High Street, and ends with slow dancing in her parlour to "Blue Moon" — what else?

After the picketing and petitioning and town talk escalated to the point that Daphne and her residents just couldn't party in peace without some delegation or other rapping on her door or stalking the raspberry bushes in her garden with cameras, Daphne decided she needed protection.

And that's when she bought the parrot.

Blanche is the most beautiful and the baddest bird this side of Turn Hill.

She's an albino.

She has long white tail feathers, with pink pin feathers. Pink eyes. A sharp beak.

Watch out for that beak, those sharp claws.

Blanche talks, of course she does. But she can say only one sentence: "Talk to me and I'll talk back."

What Charming Dave always said to Daphne, what he always says to his patients now.

The parrot lives in a wishing well in Daphne's English country garden. It swings on the bucket or perches on the peaked roof and sings to the goldfish in the cement pond: "Talk to me, Baby, and I'll talk back, oooooo, Baaaay-beeee."

Day and night the parrot guards Daphne's house. When the enemy approaches waving placards and wearing navy blue and pearls, even when the paperboy bicycles by, at the given signal from Daphne, the finger of course, the parrot lifts off from its perch on the wishing well, wings spread, and it swoops down on the intruder. Just at the moment the invader or party-pooper touches the latch on the gate or the BEWARE OF PARROT sign on the wrought-iron fence, Blanche lands on the right shoulder —always the right, never the left, because of the politics involved —and then claws digging and wings beating against the person's head, knocking perfectly decent hats right off, the parrot bites ears. It bites and nips and screeches, "TAlk awk talk." By now the invader turns in circles trying to beat off the parrot, shake off the claws. All run and holler for the police and the mounties and Elliott Ness.

The parrot pecks and squawks. Until Daphne says sweetly, "Blanche, come talk to me."

Charming Dave's mamma and the Deputy Minister of Health and His Honour the Mayor warned Dave about the parrot. They told him to wear a football helmet or earmuffs. At least cover his ears.

Charming Dave believes he needs no protection from the albino woman or her parrot.

He dons his Sherlock Holmes hat, the one Boston Barbara gave him, wraps his school scarf around his neck, then steps out of his mamma's house. "Wear your rubbers," she calls from the parlour. "It might rain."

"I'm just going next door," he says.

He sidles down the steps, slinks down the street, plucking pods from the caragana hedge. He halts before the BEWARE OF PARROT sign. He gazes at Dirty Daphne's house.

It is a clean house, no doubt about it. A fresh coat of white paint. Flower beds groomed, edging neat around the goldfish pond. The house is gabled, latticed. All the windows are open and lace curtains billow in the breeze. He imagines he sees a faint pink light in the top dormer window.

The parrot preens on the wishing well bucket. Dave wonders if the residents drop pennies into the well, wishing they didn't have to take their medicines, wishing there were a cure.

On the front porch, Daphne lounges on the swing, pushing it with one dangling and slippered foot. Her white dressing gown has fallen open: legs still long, white, tapering. Her Jean Harlow hair shines in the white sunlight. She wears dark glasses. Sips gin and lemonade. It's such a hot, white hot day. *Summertime and the livin' is easy* drifts up from her phonograph and over the drooping lilac bushes.

The residents sprawl and perch and lie about the porch. One man with a brush cut baby-talks to two beach balls, petting and patting them: his children. A girl with purple hair paints her lips bright red, peering into a silver hand-mirror. A boy with spiked orange hair has one foot up on the railing and seems to be strumming an imaginary guitar. An older woman kneels on the steps, hands folded, praying. Another man with a moustache, wearing a shiny velvet smoking jacket, counts jelly beans from one jar into another.

Charming Dave takes a deep breath and knocks on the sign. He doesn't call or wave.

Dirty Daphne bolts upright, shades her sunglasses, peering. "You?" she says.

And the parrot stops preening, it cocks its head, pink eye rolling, one foot in lift-off position.

Dave opens the gate and marches towards the wishing well.

The man with the beach balls calls, "Here kitty, kitty, kitty," to the parrot. He says to the balls, "You're so cuddly, yes you are."

"May the good Lord bless and keep you," the girl with the make-up says.

"Wanna dance?" the guitar strummer says.

And the jelly bean man says, "I win!"

The goldfish jump in the pond.

The parrot takes off. It flies at Charming Dave, white wings spread, beak opened and screeching, pink plumage lifted and fluttering. Claws curved for grasping ears.

Dave holds his left ear with his left hand and holds up his right hand. He says, "Come, Blanche. That-a-girl, come on now."

The residents jump up and down, cheering Blanche on.

"Sic'im!"

"Make him go away."

"Peck his ears off!"

Dirty Daphne looks puzzled, squints. "Is it really?" She sips her gin and lemonade, cooling her legs with a breeze she creates by swishing her silk dressing gown.

And the parrot flies.

Dave holds up his hand, an offering. He says, "Talk to me, Blanche, and I'll talk back."

The parrot takes Dave's offering in her beak and swoops around his head, circling back to the porch, to Dirty Daphne. A laurel branch, a remembrance, a promise kept?

The parrot carries to Daphne two red licorice.

The residents cheer and go into the house to dress for the party.

He doesn't notice the blue moon slide between two white clouds and turn to gold.

◆ ◆ ◆

Charmin' Dave:
    You shouldn't have told me you were born in Moose Jaw. This is for you and Daphne. Enjoy.

Estelle.
July 10,1991
(Location unkown. P.C.)

WHEN I TAKE YOU HOME AGAIN, YOU CAN DO ANYTHING YOU WANNA DO, 'CAUSE I DANCED DIRTY WITH YOU

He has Oh such Irish eyes, the very devil dancing in them. On Grand Rounds in the psychiatric ward, the Man from Moose Jaw wears mouton, double-breasted and open so I can see he has more hair on his chest than on his head. Strumming and humming, he starts off, taking me home again to see my son. Clickety-clack down the track, I lurch forward jerk back then sway from side to side down the aisle with him. Irish eyes are smiling at Virgin Mary who tells him she's waiting for her Son to come again. Elvis grooves in blue suede shows while Madonna boogies with a unicorn. Walter warbles and waltzes with sleepy sheep, he doesn't count them, he dreams with his arms around Linda who tells the Man she will be his tootsie roll. We stop before the angel boy we've come to see: he's jammin', rockin' in blue rain, calling Michael. Row the boat ashore. Meet my train. And I'm no Kathleen, but I want to be taken. Home again. Danced home with the Moose Jaw Man to the angel boy. Jumpin' with his electric bass. Dance me down. To Land's End where this crazy train rocks and jumps, it has wings, it arches over the blue, 'cause he can do anything I want him to, the devil dancing dirty in Oh such Irish eyes.

♦♦♦

Charmin' D.:
   I dreamed Paul was in Holding, but I couldn't find him. You took me on rounds, the musical tour was so frightening. I think it's all that boom-box rock Paul plays that's driving me crazy.

– Estelle G.
July 15, 1989
Regina

WATCHING ME WATCHING YOU, WAITING

He was always watching me.
 From the windows above the public dance hall I sighted him between the pillars of the Salvation Army Home. He was only half a man. He stared at his hump-toed boots.
 I kneeled on the end of my bed, elbows on the windowsill.
 He chomped an apple.
 I killed a cockroach, crushed it with the toe of my Mary-Jane. Buried it in blue powder sprinkled along the baseboard to kill roaches.
 The dwarf waved, not the first time. When it rained he wrapped himself in a black slicker. He never left his post.
 Weak-eyed Ellie in the next room moaned, rubbing herself because the organist at the Sally Ann told her to give up the evil walk with the devil.
 I pulled the shade and turned to the pimpled boy flopped on my bed.
 In the morning there were wet boot prints on the stairs, an apple core in a puddle before my door.

◆◆◆

Dave:
 This morning, in Marché Aux Fleurs I bought goat cheese from a dwarf with rind caught between his front teeth. Tonight, I remember that roach-ridden walk-up where I lived with my teacher mother. How am I now? Weak-eyed as cousin Ellie.

– Estelle.
July 30, 1991
Nice

ONLY AT NIGHT

She came out only at night.

Sophie rented the steamy room above the shoemaker's shop. All day, the backstairs creaked as they came and went, sailors, soldiers, flyboys. She squealed when she opened the door. The shoemaker heard more than glasses clinking, more than fluty music, the Jew's harp. He ground his molars. Hit his thumb with the shoe hammer.

He let her stay, languishing among her satin pillows. He needed the money.

His sewing machine droned, the leather polisher hummed. Shoe nails between his gold teeth, he hammered a new heel onto one of Sophie's sling-backs. He spat out the nails, a last tap to the heel. Mopped his balding head.

When the last man stumbled down the backstairs, after the wife had gone to her Ladies' Aid meeting at the church, the shoemaker hid in lamplight shadows.

The upstairs light winked out. A creak on the backstairs, and Sophie emerged onto the street. No bangles, silks, or rouges. She hid her bleached and teased hair under a brown felt hat. She wore a shapeless tweed coat. She carried a lumpy shopping bag, the wing of a toy airplane jutted up, between the handles. She huddled close to brick walls, picket fences, to windows of shops closed for the night.

She was always wearing down her heels.

◆◆◆

David Dear:
> I think I'm Sophie. That close to penury since I lost my job at Le Cave.
> Don't tell Paul.

E.
– August 10, 1990
Avignon

MARIELLA'S WEDDING MARCH

This time, the wedding procession was something to see.

At noon, when Marché Aux Fleurs closed in Old Nice, everyone who lived on Rue Ste. Reparate gathered at the cathedral door and formed an entourage to lead Mariella and her groom to Le Club Can-Can.

The Weeping Man was the first person to leave the square. He hadn't bathed, shaved or sobered up since the news passed from the market through the alleys: Mariella will marry on Sunday. He carried Mariella's pomeranian. He cried: *"C'est fini! Mariella est mariée!"* He staggered down the narrow passageway, weaving between café tables, weeping. Weeping. Sweat stung his pimpled forehead, dampened his greying hair and beard. He spun around and raised his arms to the sky, dropping Le Petit Marquis who scurried between tourists' feet. The Weeping Man pressed his body against the *Interdit* sign, and wailed. Le Petit Marquis snarled.

It was something to see.

The white wedding car, chauffeured by Dante, waited before the Cathedral doors. The red-finned '59 Chrysler was decorated with muslin bows and taffeta ribbons. On the hood and trunk, large flower baskets wiped out Dante's view, fore and aft.

When Mariella and her groom swept through the Square everyone sighed and said she was the happiest bride ever seen on Rue Ste. Reparate. Her white muslin blouse was unlaced to her navel, her skirt crotch-high at the front, with curtain lace trailing like a real bride's train.

"What fine rags!" Lame Letitia cried, tugging on the leash fastened to her Dobermann pinscher.

Down the street, The Weeping Man swung around the signpost, lurched to a café wall and prostrated himself upon it. He wept. He sobbed. Le Petit Marquis de Sade dashed under a table, snapping at bangled arms and foreign hands trying to pet him.

The organ grinder who looked like Rasputin on his day off from the palace opened the car door, and Mariella shoved her groom into the plush interior then climbed in too, flashing leg, her breasts bursting out of her blouse. Dante stuck his head out the side and cried, "*Allons-nous-en! Vite!*"

The mime artist led the way, in white tails and top hat, his masked face immobile, eyes glazed by a self-hypnotic trance, his robotic hip gyrations and lewd gestures prompting applause from the butcher and fish monger just closing their shops. He directed pedestrian traffic with a giant vibrator, the light on its tip flashing red for STOP, green for GO.

It too was something to see.

Next came the long-haired long-robed organ grinder who cranked the handle and played "La Vie en Rose". He was followed by Peppi, the opera singer. Fly open and rope belt loosening and threatening to release his clown pants, Peppi raised his arms and began to roar, "*O solo mio!*" He passed his wino hat as he bellowed along.

It was something to hear.

Then came Madame in royal blue silk, with a wide-brimmed hat spilling yellow honeysuckles from its crown to one bared shoulder. She linked arms with her greatest rival and one-time lover, Maestro, who wore his best leather. Not fighting over their daughter for once, they both would receive fair share of the dowry the Cincinnati Kid had paid Igor, the marriage broker.

The lettuce vendor, older sister of Lame Letitia, bared her left breast and its half-moon scar. "Monee to feed my babeeee," she wailed. She jeered at a Parisienne who handed her a mere centime. "It won't buy milk," she said. "Give me francs. Paper money."

She was followed by Yves and Georges in matching purple tank tops and sequined white pants. Each carried a caged turtle dove.

Marquis bared his teeth at Igor, the bald marriage broker, who flicked scalpdust off the shoulder of his morning coat. He carried a walking stick with an ivory knob: a nubile maiden. He brandished it at the dog, and Le Petit Marquis de Sade showed the whites of his eyes and withdrew deeper under the table.

As wide as the street and almost as long, the white wedding car rolled, slowly, like a ship cutting through a narrow inlet. Waiters hastily pulled away empty chairs and raised awnings. It swayed by applauding shopkeepers and tourists. The dwarf bounced on his six satin pillows. *"Attention!"* he yelled. *"Attention!"*

The street people called *"Bravo!"* and *"Bonneheure!"* They tossed rose petals.

That was something so sweet to smell.

The glistening bride smooched her stunned groom. He picked lint from his red sweatpants, and blushed. He turned the volume up on his ghetto blaster. The Cincinnati Kid was from the Lycée Canadienne at Ville Franche, and his real name was Lester LaMontagne.

The procession reached the corner and Le Club Can-Can, but Dante found no place to park. Self-crucified on his Wailing Wall, The Weeping Man shuddered while Dante manœuvred the car around the corner and, finding no free space on the adjoining street, continued around the bend.

The wedding car disappeared.

The Weeping Man hunched over as if an assailant's sword had thrust home. He scrambled backwards, spun around, spraying tears and sweat. Before the closing doors of Le Cave, drooling, he watched liquor bottles disappear behind shutters and iron gates. No sale until after 3:00 PM, maybe 4:00, depending on how long the vendor lunched with his new mistress. And if he joined the wedding party, maybe not until tomorrow.

It was something to mourn.

Inside Le Club, Maestro toasted Igor because this time Mariella wouldn't have to work the street for a week after the wedding. He expressed sorrow for the Cincinnati Kid who was missing such a good time.

Igor thrust his massive head out the windows. He hollered, "de Sade!". He growled at the pomeranian. "You are mine now," he said. "Just you wait."

The Weeping Man whirled around and shouted, *"Tu es un gigolo!"* He lunged and grabbed Igor's hump, sinking his ragged yellow fingernails into the exposed flesh around his neck. Igor jerked as if throwing a fit, and The Weeping Man slammed his overly large head between shutters.

Lame Letitia applauded, dropping the dog leash. The Dobermann pinscher, in a furious dust-raising dash, attacked Le Petit Marquis. The table rose up and teetered, sending wine bottles and glasses flying into laps, cutlery and *plats-du-jour* jumping and crashing onto cobblestones and empty chairs. Tourists leapt away, waiters came running; all afraid to venture under the table.

Everyone on the street heard Igor roar: "The marriage is no good! Papers, no good!"

"Dans les yeux de Dieu!" cried The Weeping Man, shoving Igor backwards, into the café. Once again he lifted his face and arms to the sky.

The pomeranian's scream sounded like that of a wailing banshee, at least that of a bedeviled whirling dervish. He whirled and leapt, confusing the Dobermann, who swung his head just as Le Marquis pounced and champed down; he made steak tartare of the Dobermann's left ear, and almost blinded him in one eye with claws as sharp as miniature daggers. The Dobermann howled.

It was something to hear.

Lame Letitia grabbed her dog's tail, pulling backwards the bloody-eyed pinscher. "Bad dog," Letitia said. "Very bad boy!"

By now, street people were tossing coins between The Weeping Man's heels. Crouching to retrieve the francs, The Weeping Man crawled across the *Interdit*, and ducked his head under the table, trying to coax out the snarling Marquis. "*Ici*," he whined. "*Ici*." He made kissing noises, caught the panting pomeranian, whose lolling tongue was now black from lapping up spilled Sambuca licorice liqueur. Then straightening, his face and neck scarlet from the effort, tears still streaming down his cheeks, The Weeping Man licked blood and licorice liqueur from the dog's lips.

And offered to sell it to the Canadians settling again at the table.

"How much?" he said. "I need money to pay for a funeral."

"I don't want the dog," the tourist said. He had a maple leaf tractor cap on backwards. He held out a palm full of coins. "Here, man. Buy yourself a drink."

"He doesn't need any more," the tourist's wife said. To her bosom she clutched a basket bulging with souvenirs: a plastic loaf of bread, a plaster of Paris model of Eze Village, a bust of Prince Rainier. She said, "He must be drunk. Or crazy."

"I am," said The Weeping Man, pocketing the money and Le Petit Marquis. He sat down across from the near-weeping woman, ordered a bottle of wine, and began to celebrate his grief.

Ah, it was a grand procession.

◆◆◆

Dear, Dear Dave:
>On the anniversary of my parents' elopement, I took part in a wedding near Marché Aux Fleurs. Yet I'm not in the story. Sorry to disappoint you. Paul excels at the Lycée in Ville Franche, but suffers the summer romance rebuffs from twin sisters with crossed eyes. We may winter here too.

>>– Your favourite correspondent
>>August 1, 1990
>>Provence

IV

WHILE THE NIGHT BIRD CALLED

*I don't believe in ghosts
but if I did I would say
the garden is haunted
not the house which reposes
in a quiet, cool peace.
First the bell, then the night
bird awakens me.
                How I wish
I could paint that sound, its unceasing
repetition: its call, its warning.*

7. *Woman Locked in the Lussan Clock Tower*
c. 1972
56 x 55 cm
Private Collection

In a poem titled "Woman Locked in the Lussan Clock Tower" Estelle Caron describes a ghost from the time of the troubadours who wanders naked at night in search of her lost Gardien lover through the gardens and alleyways of Lussan and along the stone wall of the medieval village perched on the hillside. The woman, "wrapped in widow's weeds like heavy dark plumage," tells a young pregnant wife of an ancient Provencal superstition that a guest must never leave an iron exposed to the light of day or it will bring misfortune to the woman of the house. And while Christophe in the single bed next to hers "thrashed in the throes of a dream I dread," Estelle remembers she left the old flat-iron on the board after pressing her husband's shirt. After her husband's death, the artist insisted he never would have died if she hadn't forgotten to put the iron away. In the poem, the woman with child "hurled the Gardien's trident/through the Clock Tower's window." And freed the woman's blue spirit.

In the painting, the artist sits on a Victorian footstool, in the left corner, bare back to the viewer, watching her husband/lover sleep in a stone-walled boudoir with a low cavernous ceiling. At her bare feet, an overturned vase spills dry strawflowers, withered lavender, and in the middle of a spreading puddle of milky water, the singular bloom of one yellow rose. Hidden moonlight illuminates him, the muscular twist of torso, dark mossy chest hair, a yellow hooked nose in sharp contrast to green-blue masses of feathery hair. He lies on his back, one ankle caught behind the curve of the other knee. His right hand, balled into a fist, fits the soft impression left by her departed body. His right arm is arched over his head, the claw fingers tearing at the lace on her pillow. Yet his head is turned away from her side of the bed, facing the high window.

At the top of the painting, as if the dungeon-like walls and ceiling are transparent, we see a dark garden of cypress, plane and mulberry. A blue-black night bird with yellow beak opened in a cry swoops towards the Lussan Clock Tower at the top left corner. There, the same hidden moonlight that illuminates the lover/husband reveals a small, child-like, unclothed woman with long, wild and tangled tresses hurling an iron at the face of the clock, which has no hands.

8. The Night Bird's Warning
   (Lussan, July 1, 1972)

There's a night bird, only one, that begins to sing after the Clock Tower bell has bonged its twelve midnight strokes, a strange echo of those chimes. I don't believe in ghosts, but if I did, I would say that the garden is haunted, not the house which reposes in a quiet, cool peace. First the bell, then the bird, awakens me every night. How I wish I could paint that *sound*, its unceasing repetition, its call, its warning. The bird can only utter two notes, the first like an exhaled breath, the second inhaled, not a raspy, wheezy sound, but closer to a double-cry when the wind is knocked out of the stomach. The first strong, sharp *Bing*, like F-sharp on a penny whistle, made me think of silver metal on stone, of a Roman coin dropped onto a limestone slab on Pont Du Gard. The second note is closer to B-flat, lower, softer, yet tinnier. I imagined a mother bird trying to teach a squab how to sing, but the babe had a sunflower seed caught in its throat.

The night bird's call finally drifted away, towards the Clock Tower.

All night, Christophe thrashed in the throes of a dream I dread, but I dared not wake him for fear I'd prevent a resolution to his nightly struggle. He slept so rarely now, I knew he needed whatever rest even troubled sleep can bring.

I tried to read Zola's *L'Oeuvre*, which Christophe had been pressing upon me for some days. And then, while the night bird chimed its warning, I discovered Christophe in Zola's description of Claude:

> *This was his chaste passion for the flesh of a woman, a foolish love of nudity desired and never possessed, an impotence to satisfy himself, to create this flesh so much that he dreamed of holding it in his two bewildered arms. These women whom he drove away from his atelier, he adored in his paintings — there he caressed them and violated them, desperate that through his tears he would not have the power to make them as beautiful and vibrant as he desired.*

And then I began to understand the raving when I dropped and broke a vase on the stone floor, the windmilling arms when I scorched a white shirt, the disgust when I mispronounced a word or spat out the French *R* instead of swallowing it. And oh, the groans and snuffling that accompanied the twisting of my arms, the painful spreading of my hip bones, the pressure on my face when I failed to turn my head quickly enough and was smothered by his hairy chest. And finally his tears when my mouth was too small to take in all of him and I choked, then gagged.

Because of the dry summer heat that never lifts even at night, we had retreated to the bedroom just off the summer kitchen. Once a wine cellar, the thick stone walls and arched ceiling created a cave. I looked at Christophe and saw at once a reversal of Manet's *Olympia* that was damned by 19th century critics for the indecency of a thin nude courtesan waiting in her boudoir with her black servant and cat for her lover. Then I remembered Cézanne's response, "A modern *Olympia* (*The Pasha*)," in which the heavily and darkly clothed artist gazes (from afar) with temptation at a nude woman in her gauzy bed, on her side and crouched against the wall, knees drawn up to her chest, while fanned by an unclothed black serving woman. I looked at Christophe again and wanted a woman's perspective on all of this, an answer, rather than an allusion or a cruel joke.

Secretly, at night, in that cavernous boudoir, I began to paint furiously, by the light of an old lantern placed on the floor under the barred window.

While the night bird called, called.

AFTER TWENTY-FIVE YEARS, STILL WORKING IT OUT

Oh Baby, he doesn't laugh like that when he's awake. Curled under the covers, he chuckles in his sleep, and it's making you crazy. When he slept on his back and snored you cured him by pinching his nose, and now you try everything, even pat his bum with a broom, but you can't stop his snuffling and snorting. His shoulders shake slightly as if he's sharing a secret under the sheet the way he did with you when he could stay awake long enough to romp. You've just got to know what's so funny. You lie still, hoping he'll talk in his sleep and give it away, but he never does.

He always told you everything, but every morning he says he can't remember his dreams. He says he's happy with you, that's all. But you're sure he dreams of a four-breasted woman who neighs, one with eight legs who can fly, or worse: someone you know. The fluffy secretary who makes up in hair what she lacks in height. The gas jockey who can't zip up her jacket. Or the girl with incurable giggles who slaps bums with the towels she hands out at the Y. You always said if he ever cheated you would know by the way he walked down the hall: all the leg action from the knees down.

You try to tickle him awake to catch him in the act, but that only makes him chortle louder. He sleeps with the sheet over his head. You slide out of bed, creep around to his side, kneel on the floor, carefully oh so slowly lift the sheet and stick your head under it. Nose to nose. His twitches. Ears wiggle, bottom lip wobbles, Adam's apple bobs, chuckle chuckle, chort. He has one grey hair on his chest. And then you know how you can stop him from having such a good time without you.
  In his sleep you are laughing.

❖❖❖

D.L.K.:

    While visiting my mother she told me an impossible story about the 25th wedding anniversary she never had. I guess it's in the genes. I'm fossilizing too soon, but closer to the final canvas.

E.G.C.
– Easter, 1985
Saskatoon

THE WAY SHE GOES

The girl in the elevator will never have a name, a face. She will be remembered for her black patent leather jacket, the sheen of her hair and the way it ripples and flows, like dark water. Four silent men want to touch the soft leather, her hair: the Japanese business man who drops his briefcase; the Texas oilman who grips his steerhorn belt buckle; the Ottawa lawyer who picks a boil on his reddened neck; and the oldest man whose bottom lip droops. He sneezes and his nose hair waves like red ant legs. The woman next to him, a new grandmother, gives him the elbow. That's just what men do, but no one ever looks at her like that, not now. He ducks his head sideways and combs his thin hair with his fingers so it flips to the wrong side and bares his flaky scalp. The doors slide open on 2 and the leather girl bounces out, hair swinging. The older woman says, "Nice jacket." The Texan says, "That's the way she goes." She's left behind a scent the older woman can name: *Remembrance*. Of how all heads turn and look up at her, in white patent leather maxi-coat and go-go boots, descending slowly down the staircase built into the side of a mountain, down to a garden of philodendron and birds of paradise and monkey puzzle trees. Her platinum hair gleams in the torch light, flows in graduated, geometric lengths that graze her shoulders. At the bottom, he waits in white suede shoes, twilled duck trousers, a royal blue smoking jacket. He takes her arm, guides her behind the party tent, grips her shoulders and swings her around, backing her against the chain-link fence. You blow in here, he says, and knock me out. That's just the way she goes. An old woman now, with no name, no face.

◆◆◆

Doctor Dave:
> You asked me how I see myself twenty years from now. This morning on an elevator in Toronto I saw me in 1972 and then at the turn-of-the-century. The old man in the story is Christophe if he had lived. You had to ask.
>
> Estelle.
– May 1, 1985
Enroute to France

SAFE SEX

Anything can happen in Japanese *tatami* rooms.

Inside: a sunken floor, raised table and chrysanthemum centrepiece, cushions to lounge upon, bamboo walls holding and enfolding. A silkscreen print, the delicate touch of a brush, its stroke so light: a beautiful woman in kimono brought in a rickshaw to the mandarin's house.

He sits cross-legged on a cushion, you on his left side. Hot *saki*, he holds the tiny cup to your lips, you sip, inhaling, then suddenly the hot *saki* rushes through your arms, your body, legs. It closes your eyes.

You feel bared, the silk of his skin brushing as he slides his left arm behind you, not touching, not yet. You swing your legs around, stretch them out, and lean against him, your head on his shoulder. You are clothed in chyrsanthemum petals. You hear the parchment-panelled doors slide open, and words soft as rain.

Chopsticks between his fingertips balanced just so, he drops into your mouth: *sushi, sashami, wasabi,* shredded carrot, tiny shrimp. Spice smell, ginger hot on your tongue.

You float in clear jasmine-scented water, steaming now, your skin, his, oiled and smooth, heat emanates from his heaving chest, passes from his palm into the fan of your hand. The hollow of his neck, the rounded shoulder, the length of his left arm, its fine golden hair. You will never open your eyes again, lift your head, move. Enfolded, you wait. Lips parting. More hot *saki*. On your tongue: *futomaki,* seaweed, *te-maki,* soya sauce. Lobster now, dipped in butter. Black bean sauce. Green snow pods. Almond slivers. Every breath deeper now, the rise and fall of his chest, the rhythm of his torso as it moves forward, back, his left cheek round and smooth and hot against yours. *Tempura.* The tang, the hot and sour, plum. So sweet so sour, pineapple.

The parchment doors slide open, close, open, a fan folds into your right hand, your tiny feet bound. Falling, floating, turning. Slowly, you feel your body lowered, your head sinks into the cushion. You hear the slide and click of the doors. You open your eyes, lift your heavy body, silk clinging to your moist skin. Then rising, stumbling, faltering on your knees, you crawl to the doors, open them to the cold air, the white light.

◆◆◆

Dave:
> Thanks for dinner and going with me to see Christophe's childhood home in Montreal. I'm trying to paint it, but clearly cannot see the boy he was, the face becoming Paul's on canvas. So I write this only for you.

Estelle.
– May 15, 1985
Provence

THE PAST, UNDONE

She never wanted to go back and do it all again, undo the past. She waited too long, he did, failed to capture and hold the moment. If she had known their first night would be the last, she wouldn't have let him go. He insisted on seeing her to her door, both confessing their fear of the elevator, of enclosure, of falling. Her mother's apartment was empty, the movers gone, except for the bed in the alcove promised to a friend. He sidled through the door behind her, then inspected the remains of her mother's life, halted with her at the glass doors overlooking the swift-running river. He didn't want to leave, she knew that, knew he was waiting for her take his hand and lead him to the bedroom. He stalled, she hesitated, and then she took him back down the elevator, laughing at their fear, he leaping out when the doors opened, her last sight of him, and then he was gone.

This once quick-footed man leans heavily on a cane, shaking and weeping. His wife has brought him in a vis-à-vis park carriage with hickory wheels and brass fittings. Leather seats. So that's what she looks like: a tired Raggedy Ann. She cannot slow him down, not even now. Take him back, she says. She steps aside, and together they watch him hasten back to the carriage. Ready. And then she's flying to him, up for the ride. Beside him in the back. The horse's hind legs bunch, its head swinging 'round, it rears, pushing. Backwards. Runs now. On a paved road that turns to gravel to sandy soil to dust. Back and back, so swiftly, spruce and poplar swishing by, the fields yellowing, lightening, greening.

    The river ahead, curving around, turning back on itself.
    Unravelling.
    Now undone.

♦♦♦

Dave:

    How wonderful of you to take time to see me. I'm so glad, too, that your paper was well-received at the conference. Closing my mother's apartment was — so hard — all those photos from the past, now she has no memory of them. The past. It can be undone. So you must put that moment in the elevator right. The next time. Before it's too late.

Estelle.
– April 10, 1989
Saskatoon

PANSIES

She doesn't care what he does as long as he doesn't touch her pansies. He clangs pails together in the tool shed. Barefooted, shirt sleeves rolled up with elastic armbands, suspenders slipped down over his shoulders slapping against his baggy pants. He mutters: fire fire fire. She hides behind the hedges in her pansy garden. Blue skirt pinned up between her legs, she squats, snipping withered petals. When he could remember names he always said she should have been called Violet, but that wasn't what made her tear out the phlox and petunias and sweet peas then fill the beds with pansies. They cut out her womb, the deadly smell of root-rot. Then, shaved, spread-eagled, the heavy large cone with its black head aimed between her legs. The map they made of her privates, the targets, a military manoeuvre. There were others, how many she doesn't know, but five lived to tell her, Yes me too. They were the first saved. He drags the hose along the lawn, hollering, Douse it douse it! With her watering can she sprays the velvety blossoms, the tiny heads lift and turn, soft silky petals fluttering. He drags the garden hose into the house, shouting, Fire in the basement! He wasn't always like this. She strokes silky petals. Red and purple and yellow and black. They burned away her labia. Oils and salves no balm, she lies at night beside him, iced teabags secreted between her legs. The back door flings open, his engineering books fly out and rise and arch, pages like opening wings. Flapping, then dive-bombing trash cans. His eyes are crazed, as if he can see beyond the house, the garden. Don't worry, we'll lick this sucker! Get her under control. He disappears inside. And turns the hose full blast against the window panes, his voice like a foghorn or no — a drowning man's. He probably turned on all the taps in the house too. Maybe it will fill up and float away. She doesn't care, take it all, let it go, as long as he doesn't drown her pansies. No one touches her pansies.

♦♦♦

My dear Paul:
    I'm working on a new canvas: your Great-Aunt Erica's story, but I can't send this to her, not even to Linnaea. Strange, how your grandmother is only two rooms away from your Uncle Chester in the Special Care Unit. No longer can one recognize the other. Let's plant pansies for them.

– Lovingly, Mum
May 24, 1989
Regina

V

WOMEN DIVING INTO WATER

Spread on the cavern floor
like a child, with cheeks cupped in hands,
he gazed at his collected evidence
of the water nymph:

> *a blue feather*
> *an apricot half, with teeth marks*
> *the broken neck of a bottle*
> *of Montserrat lime juice*
> *a shredded red ribbon.*

9. *Women Diving into Water*
  (*The Bathers*)
  c. 1972
  Pencil, watercolour and gouache on paper
  12.7 x 12.1 cm
  Saskatchewan Arts Board Permanent Collection, Regina

The title, likely taken from Cézanne's 1867 painting in bodycolour, may be a private allusion to a moment of inspiration since Estelle Caron's painting bears no resemblance to Cézanne's. In 1991, she renamed it *The Bathers*.

Though the wheatfield superimposed on the cloudless blue of the prairie sky and the garden of hollyhocks, gladioli, sunflowers, Oriental poppies, and yellow begonias from the artist's Regina home were painted in after the death of her husband, the central figures, the bathers in the landscape of Provencal mulberry, crooked olive trees, and a dark vineyard scorched by a merciless sun are obviously the Carons at Maison Fell in Lussan.

Once again, the disembodied artist's presence is felt, for her footprints lead from the clawfoot tub to a yellow masonry wall where it looks like she tried but failed to pass through it and, with a flip of an eyelet slip and the kick of a bare foot, vanished to the left where, we assume, she wheeled about and painted the bathers in the tub. It reminds us of *Disappearing Woman* by Margaret Vanderhaeghe, without that artist's evocative simplicity.

From the viewpoint of the top, right hand corner where a causeway connects the Canadian prairie to the Provencal plain, the eye is drawn, down, to the lovers lying in a clawfoot bathtub.

Flung on a mulberry bush is a wispy blue dress, swollen like a curtain full of breeze, while his ochre-yellow suit is neatly folded beside it. With strong curving brushstrokes, the artist has laid on layer upon layer of dark blue-grey tones shot with red, reminiscent of Van Gogh's landscapes.

Submerged, on his back, Christophe Caron cradles his wife, a full-blown nymph, with a clear allusion to Venus. His left arm falls over the side of the tub, but his right hand encircles her swollen belly, washing the pubic area. Both hands have been replaced by yellow claws. Her head rests on his right shoulder, her hair a mass of thorny rose vines. Her left arm, parallel to his, holds a fan of black and white feathers which appear to be tangled in or metamorphosing from his hair. His cheek presses against hers. While her eyes are closed, his are stark, bold, and widened by surprise — or fear — that intense stare found in Cézanne's self-portraits. The profile of the lover, an eagle head, is obviously taken from the Roman eagle standard.

In a later portrait of the engineer on the Pont du Gard, the man, part eagle part goat, wears a centurion's tunic. His belt buckle bears the insignia of the phallus engraved on the viaduct, the Hare or Gopher that, according to legend, was hurled with such force by Satan that its imprint was left, like a fossil, in the stone. It is believed that the phallus symbol was represented on Roman monuments to protect the builders from the Evil Eye. (cat. figure 24.)

10. Farewell to Pont du Gard
(Lussan, September 1, 1972)

In Lussan, your father hid in the cave of the cellar at night and drove me away from the natural vegetation into the aqueduct's canals during the day.

For five weeks, morose and increasingly frantic, he dragged me the length of the canal, from its captage point at the springs of Eure and Airan to its distribution station at Nîmes, over rocky hillsides, down broken slopes, through ravines, and across streams. Even if I hadn't experienced the usual nausea, fatigue, swollen ankles and backache, the daily jaunts would have been arduous, sometimes treacherous for me. There was a plague of mosquitoes, horse-flies, gnats, and soon I was covered with bites, scabs, sores. Though it's only a short distance from Lussan to Nîmes, each day we covered different ground, a key opening or station or quarry. From the Vers limestone quarries to Sernhac where the aqueduct disappears underground, he chipped at the waterproof coating, collected calcium deposits, bits of shale and fossils, and scrounged for Roman coins.

At night, he even tried to recreate the red waterproof coating that Pliny the Elder said was made of chalk, wine, fig juice and pork fat, though he well knew it was merely iron oxide.

I began to dread each sunrise when the night bird ceased to sing. I bargained for respite: "You brought me here to create, and now I must have equal time for my work."

More and more manic, before the mastery and precision of the aqueduct, he searched for evidence of watergods — nymphs, demons, and dragons — that Celto-Ligurians believed guarded the dark caverns and basins and springs. "You must come," he said, "you must see what's hidden in the land. Then you paint it."

Soon, I was holding him back, seeking shelter from the blazing heat, nearly fainting, needing to stop for rest, and sometimes I was just afraid. If we ventured too far into the canal we might never return. "You seem to forget," I said, "that there's a third person, your child, to think of."

And he barely heard me, shushing me, "Listen! Can you hear her?", and he'd cock his head as if the waterfall's rush contained the song of a sprite.

Finally, exhausted, I refused to venture to the station at Nîmes. "It's the last day," I said. "Just go. End it. I can't go any further."

"Today I find her," he said. "I've followed her trail, her scent, she's not so far — " Spread on the cavern floor like a child, with cheeks cupped in hands, he gazed at his collected evidence of the water-nymph: a blue feather, an apricot half with teeth marks, the broken neck of a bottle of Montserrat lime juice, a shredded red ribbon.

The day before we were to return home, he drove to Nîmes alone. I can't know what he found there, apart from the baths and basin and Roman ruins.

Now, I believe he realized he wasn't a Roman engineer reincarnated, and that he could never build his dream of a causeway.

He returned late, long past the night bird's first cry, his jeans torn at the knees, rivulets of sweat streaking like rivers down the crusty smear of chalkdust on his face. His fingernails were ragged and bleeding. He dumped his satchel on the kitchen table. And announced: "Tommorow. Farewell to Pont du Gard. And it's done."

MISSING

I find you in the strangest places. Gathering mangoes in Montserrat, learning a rune in Stockholm, refurbishing a roadster in Marseille, walking on water in Provence. And now here, on a French island, missing you, I stalk the beach and fume at the wind filling the footprints you left in sand dunes. The backwash sweeps clean the message you scrawled with a stick on the shore: No story-painting here. I am not the first or only woman to expose her breasts to the sun, it just feels like it. I am no lover romping nude in the sea, not without you. Buffeted by crosswinds, I hover along the shore, neither missing nor missed. As if lashed to a mizzen mast, the bronze and buxom figurehead protecting the ancient vessel from the curse of the gods as it plunges into deep troughs, I sight you looming far ahead, not yet an old man, the land demanding your return. I stalk you, circling nearer, nearer. Oh yes, it's you, no mistaking the triangle of women, languishing nude around you: long lines of legs, bared breasts. No story-painting here. But no, you are really somewhere else, far away. Gathering mangoes, carving new runes, building bridges over water.

◆ ◆ ◆

Dave:
    If you miss me write right back. Here I've found a
    peaceful island where I may reflect and dream, but
    haunted I am by Christophe.
    Everywhere.

                                         Estelle.
                                    – February, 1985
                                    The Caribbean

LADYBOAT

The Canadian woman launches a yellow sunfish through the boiling backwash into the blue Caribbean.

No one sunning on the black lava beach notices her departure.

Wobbling, her flat pale feet planked loosely on the board, she grips the bar, not knowing how to sail close to the wind. The yellow sail captures a gust of wind here, snatches at a pocket there. Her cauliflower skin prickles, white in the high sun. She stands tall now, trying to tack and cross. The sunship threatens to broach, to founder.

No one on the rocky point notices how unsteadily the sunfish takes to the wind. No one oiling and peeling and basking on the beach says, She's too old. The Montserrat boys do headstands and push-ups and kick up like donkeys around a golden girl from the sunflower state. They don't even see the older paler woman.

There she goes!

The tradewinds from the Atlantic side of the island scale the mountain, pick up speed over Salem and Olde Towne, gathering, blowing full, prevailing. She's close, close to the wind, heeling now, closer to the sun.

The Ladyboats, named for the women who waited, sailed from Halifax to Boston to Barbados. Lady Nelson. Lady Drake. Lady Rodney. One took her lover with it. A mere midshipman, he was *her* lord, her admiral. If you control the Caribbean you control the world, he said. Then he was lost at sea.

And forty years later she finds his place in the sun. The plantation wall, the street behind a street where five families wailed at dawn when the news broke with its rising: the Ladyboat was torpedoed by a German submarine, five Montserrat deckhands gone down with her.

SEARCHING FOR THE NUDE IN THE LANDSCAPE

The sunsurfer, that yellow sunfish, heels. The woman grips the bar, steady, her head lifted to the sun, steady, her eyes fixed on the line where the sky meets the sea and the sun slides into the deep. Her arms ache, but she's used to hauling and chopping and pulling. Her legs buckle and her bare feet slip, but she holds fast. Fixed on that horizon, disappearing. Crossing now, tacking, the bow lifting and nosing between a ketch and a catamaran built for racing before headwinds. An English Captain shouts something she cannot hear above the mourning wind. She cannot see him, yellow light blinding, saltspray stinging. Tears.

She doesn't turn the sailbar, tack and return.

Her course is set for the disappearing sun, the exploding sky.

◆ ◆ ◆

D.L.K.:
>You were right. There is a story
>here. Everywhere a familiar,
>a nude in every landscape.

E.G.C.
– February 15, 1986
Montserrat

THE MERMAID IN CHANCE'S POND

Dat sireen in the crater up-bove Chance's Point.

She dere, dung in da bottom. She got no corn-row hair, no headkerchief. She wil'. She slinky and sultry and sneaky. She just lie dung dere, combin' her long hair, and she can really sing, you know. She sing to fishermon and turn he boat upside dung. She call me mon Easter, and she take away key to he brains. He lost he head ober dat mermaid. He say Easter Monday he dive dung, into Chance's Pond, and he steal her comb.

"Fait' to God," he say, "I see her."

I neber see her. I too scairt to go up-bove dat mountain. You climb up dere and you get stone bruise. Poppalolo ants bite you. You get soppin' wet.

The weather set up all the time ober dat mountain. Dark clouds hide de peak and sireen inna Pond. Once, she sing to pilot like he a skylark and play fool wid her. She slack, she slut-dawg, she out-light woman. She call to pilot and he no see Chance's Point onna count of bad wedder and clouds wrap around dat peak, something wrong with he instruments too, so he think he comin' dung to Antigua, only it dat green serrated mountain Columbus fust see and like so much he name this island Montserrat. Dat flyer, he hear gel sing dung in Chance's Pond, he see her combin' her long hair, and he bash upside mountain and kill eberybody inna plane. They buried inna deadyard, but dat skylark, he fall dung inna Pond and he soul stay dere with that sometimish naked sireen. He jumbie now.

And me scairt.

Me mon, Easter, he go Chance's Pond and he come home wid snow in he brains.

He one broken stick.

He kick up like donkey.
He don't know he arm from he elbow.
He say he crazy 'bout that sireen. He steal her comb.
He no piss wid me no more, pay me no attenshun. Me got a mind to kill somebody.

When me catch meself me know he akimbo he hurt me. "No make me have to chase up de mountain to come look for you," I say to Easter. "It coahl up dere, I got no hambrilla to cubber me hair."

What I goan do widdout me mon?

First to commence, I throw bone dice when I take up wid Easter.

He no spree-boy. He buckle down and do job. He clean pools for ex-pats in Olde Towne and Salem and Woodlawn. He bring me ginger stick and sugar-cane and sometime peppermint from Plymouth. He dress up in he best clothes and oh, he scent good. He boot-a-boot like he got nobody but he got me. I brimmin' full of love for he but he brimble me. Dat pickney a real badorashun. He drink Bay rum. He no abuse me. He just too common wid heself.

We no tie up togedda, no wedding, but we get pickney boy togedda. Then we get pickney gel.

I buckle down and do job. I clean house for ex-pats in Olde Towne and Salem and Woodlawn, for fat alien tourist womans.

Easter do no job no mo'. He drink Bay rum alla day. He go out, dung town, and he make one big ole halloobooloo. He toad drunk. He no ring no banjo bell wid me now. But we make anudder pickney. He fall dung, brag about dat, dondo-head.

"We no play dolly house," I say. "You buckle dung and do job, directly so."

"Sho," he say. But he drink mo' Bay rum.

One foreday marnin' old fowl cock frazzle out.

Easter gone for long time and he come home diffrunt.

He fall inna door mout'. He all dolls up in he bes' clothes but he soppin' wet. He white as alien tourist mon.

"Easter," I say, "You sick, boy? Goat water cookin' in de tinning." He like dat stew, but not today.

He just floops down heself and dry wipe he face and armpits. "Fait' to God," he say, "I see her." He draw cross on he palm and he raise he hand above he head. "I swear," he say. "You do wha' you like."

"Me fix you up."

"Turn you coat pan de wrong side an' go look foo youself," he say. He bad talk me. He not heself. He cantenshush. He touchous.

I put me hands on me hips and cack-up me foot on he chair and not care if me show me blooma under me skirt. "Me hit me broom on you nose. A wheh you be?"

"A dat eat you out," he say. "You envious."

"Come see me and come lib wid me are two diffrunt things. Who you see? Who you wid, boy? You crack-headed. We got pickney togedda."

"You cut you eye afto me," Easter say. He teeth chitter. I hold he head while he throw up in de tensil. He lay he kinky head on me tittie, and I feel he feverish. Shiva all ober. He say he got jambie legs, they just dancing to be off to dat mountain some mo'. He hot then he coahl. It like he got dinghy fever. It like malaria. Doctah shop no help. Easter crabbish and cross, not heself. He floops he arm at me and push me away.

"When you own lice bite you," I say, "he bite you for true. A wheh you be? Who you see?"

"Wha' you talk about?"

"Who go wid? Not me, for true."

"You bang you mouth too much."

Easter no quick boy with de gels. But he give me pravikashun. We never quall befo'. He belly quake, he so hungry. Me know he akimbo. Me mind tell me he suck salt. I give he fever grass tea and bush tea too. I hold he chin so he swallow it down good. "Feel bedda?"

After me done feed he, he turn around and cuss me. He one thieving dog. "Me no want nutten from you," he say. "You noodo!" He zoops pass me. He wil'. He clutch he belly. "It wuk me," he say. Outside, he drop he draaz. He give me he backside, he say, and now he get worse. He so mean.

"Wash you mout'," I say. "You no tullie me no mo.'"

We bust up for sho' now. Me boot me head against de door with him. "G'wan!" I holler after him. "Go away."

"Na-haaa!" He laugh. "I hafoo go Chance Bay." He zip up he pants and come back inna house. He floops down again and dry wipe he mouth wid me headkerchief. "I make canfeshun," he say. "Me canshunce bodder me."

Me no trust he now. He a setting fowl.

"How you mean?"

"No ask me no lawya question," he say. "Shut up you mout' an' lissen. Siddung!"

"Shut you mout' you catch no fly." I lissen, no siddung. And he tell me he take me jaagie-bundle, kittle drum, saltfish, Bay rum, and he bum ride as far as de road to up-bove Chance's Point. Then he run bird speed, climb three more hour till he come to high air and clouds thinnin' out, and he go fish in Chance's Pond. He belly quake he so hungry. He wan' fish-roe bad.

"Me no catch fish-roe," he say. "Me catch mermaid."

What he say, it rank it stink so bad. "Dog dead wid you," I say. "Dis end of you."

"Why me come home?"

"You need you crocus bag, you raincoat?"

"She coo really sing, you know."

I see he coonivin'. He got cow itch. I chalk what he tell me. He got cheesey-foot when he take off he shoes. He rank all obber. He give me bad word, he pull on me earbag.

"Cool you heart. Cool out undah tree."

"Cumma," he say. He pat me knee like he spect me to siddung. I coo give he a stick-lash instead. He a pickney-head and he wear a tam but he ugly now. Me his woman no mo'. He love no good slut-dawg, a sireen, and he got bad fever obber her. He one sick boy he think I smooch now.

"Cumma!" he say again. "One las' time." And he look so poory I say, "Maybe one las' time," and I siddung, careful, no cuddle up. He arm me gentle, and he say me hair look fine all hung down. "Doan make corn-row no mo'," he say.

"It look wil' dat way."

He say he like it loose. He ease up a liddle and pull something oudda he pocket. It silver. It smell fishy. It a comb, and he say, "Hole back you hair wid dis." He say he go, right to bottom of Chance's Pond and he steal mermaid comb just foo me. He say I bagga-leg like her.

"You not so ugly," he say.

And Easter, he a pickney boy with a wooly tam, but he Irish. He got green eyes. When I look deep, I see that sireen in he eyes, wid her long hair. I see meself.

Me coo really sing, you know.

Me turn me coat on de wrong side, and me and Easter, we skedazzle togedder, rippin'-speed.

God forgive me and pardon me if it ain't true.

They but one mon and one woman in Chance's Bay.

◆◆◆

Paul:
> This is a true island myth. Soon you will see the modern version, the island boys cycling to the top of the mountain on Easter Sunday. The winner, the first to dive into Chance's Pond, will find the Mermaid's Comb. I'll meet your plane in Antigua.
>
> – Lovingly, Mum
> March 1, 1986

ONE LOVE SONG
CAN ONLY LEAD TO ANOTHER

The chaperon doesn't know where to look.

In the Vue Pointe Hotel bar, the green-eyed Montserratian sings the blues, his heavy thighs spread on a high stool, his shirt unbuttoned unbelievably low, right down to his buckle, and the chaperon just doesn't know where to look.

She doesn't hate men. She was married once and didn't like the institution much, that's all. The daughter of an evangelist, she has a responsibility, and she always tells her girls about men. "The MEN," she says. "All they ever think about is SEX. If you dive too deep you'll rupture and come up with the bends."

Her charges, both fourteen and budding bright as birds of paradise weaving along the edge of the open air window, perch on bar stools, the blonde one lingering too long there. She orders Cokes from the bartender who shows her the whites of his eyes. The chaperon's girls don't have enough moral fibre, not like the chaperon who is as tough and stringy as overcooked christophene and as starchy as plantain. She has to be on the lookout for trouble. Oh why is she thinking of green bananas? Someone broke into her room last night and left one of those disgusting decadent vibrators under her pillow. Whatever happened to short-sheeting?

The chaperon sips her after-dinner tea, longs for a rum punch, but she has to set an example, and doesn't want to get fired. She can't see the singer's face, so dark in the corner. He lounges on his stool. Dark drooping leaves above him. His left foot slides and beats out the rhythm, those pants so tight along his thick thighs, just like Belafonte.

She can't bear to look.

His song is so suggestive, she's certain she heard the word for copulation, *It's been so long, angel falling too close to the ground.* Gazing around the room doesn't help. A young Brit has his hand right on a bushy blonde's thigh. Another girl with breasts bulging out of her blouse bounces so they swing like red hams from a market hook. So much nuzzling and eye-gazing everywhere. You almost breathe IT in the air.

She fidgets with the school crest on her navy jacket. Her legs feel so heavy and sticky, her stockings damp and steaming, her feet swelling in her navy pumps; she'd chuck them, but she has that responsibility to her charges, to their parents, to her father, and to herself, never mind the weather.

The March moon rides high, the stars so different in this hemisphere. Craning her neck to look out the window, she can't find the hunter's belt, *Oh falling too close to the ground.*

Flamboyant pods, black and long and heavy with seeds frighten her, but she sneaks another look at the singer. His tongue darts out and around his lips. It's as pink and sticky-looking as the hibiscus stamen. Or is it pistil? Dear heaven, she can't remember her basic biology. She just can't look at the singer, at those shifting rolling shoulders, those hands plucking strings. His palms, white as the underbelly of a fish, bother her so much.

She pats her wavy hair. Oh why are all the girls blonde and buxom, all coupled with boys in white pants, boiled but not from the Island sun? Couples everywhere. Even the seniors, the expatriots from retirement villas, are carried away by the song, sprung into spasms of something bygone. One man with mottled scaly skin, an old iguana, swoons toward his wife who sank hip deep into the hot *sousfrère* and now swings her bandaged leg from her wheelchair. Something prehistoric here, the way the old iguana waggles his wattled chin in time to the song, *Oh, desperado.*

She doesn't know where to look.

And oh my goodness, the singer seems to be looking right at her. She crosses her legs at the ankles the way a lady must sit.

He seems to be singing right to her, *Oh come to your senses and let someone love you before it's too late.* She clutches her purse, snapping it open and shut, open and shut.

Desperately, she looks for her charges: there they are, still at the bar. She must pluck them away, save them from those charming boys. Half-Irish, half-African, with their green eyes and golden skin, Gaelic mixed into an African dialect so they never speak, they SING. Their African legs stretch long from high round rumps; they never walk to market, they SLINK around volcanic mountains. Women wearing turbans carry bundles on their heads, and old men ride donkeys, but those young men with wool caps just sing and dance along *your forest waters, your shining sands.*

He's still doing it! Singing to her!

She'll never forget this.

Never forget the tree frog, its throat swelling to twice its body size, an enormous pouch, a crooning for its mate from the crotch of a banyan.

Don't panic.

Don't look at him.

She flutters, waving at a waiter wearing an Emerald Isle vest, until he brings her the tab. He asks her to write her room number on it. Then she rises, picks at her skirt clinging to her buttocks, and strides to the bar where she takes each charge by a padded shoulder, and pulls them away from the boys. She marches them towards their rooms in the bungalows on either side of the pool, absolutely certain she sees the waiter give the green-eyed singer her chit with her room number on it.

The singer winks at her and slips the paper into his belt buckle, not missing a beat, *let someone love you,* his voice wild Montserrat honey, full and round as a ripe mango.

She feels like an empty hammock slung between lime trees.

He will sing at her window, later, come to her dark under the moon. He will slide his lithe body over her windowsill, *before it's too late.*

And then, what ever will she do?

◆◆◆

Dave:

> I won't last long at this job. I fall for green eyes, once each hour. Here, the title says it all. For Paul who thinks I should go out more. The study is of the Vue Point Hotel.
>
> Estelle.
– March, 1986
Montserrat

A NIGHT OWL, AN HIBISCUS, A MUD HEN

You should be glad for the prickly pear hedges he raises between you. Walls you're set on walking through if you can't jump them.

The walls are real, concrete hotel walls.

And you, a woman who never went to a man's room.

From the first night, What am I doing here? translates into Why am I in this room alone, so alone, in this double bed?

He earns your trust every night when he marches you to your door and leaves you. You try to make him think you aren't a dangerous woman, which of course you are, oh yes.

You can't sleep. Not with him in the room next door, probably munching on the leftover Chinese food you had for dinner. No, you can't sleep, your bed too wide too long, though you curl into a corner, nesting, fluffing your feather pillow, wiggling like a mud hen burrowing.

You were little and quick; now you're languid and slow.

You eat for comfort, feel guilty, say you hate it but you love the indulgence.

You are a night owl, crying the hours.

You press your face into the soft red heart of an hibiscus.

◆◆◆

Dear F.R.C.P:
    How can I be alone when I have my art, my son. And you to inspire me?

                                E.C.G.
                            – Winter, 1986
                            The Caribbean

WHILE TREE FROGS SING

At home, there is only snow.

Once, on the road between cities, I heard the high call of tree frogs. It was the wind whistling through the antennae of the cellular car phone. Once, on a Maui beach, where you are now, I found a horny tree frog in the crotch of a banyan tree, its throat swelled to twice its body size.

Here, the airport is riotous with greying lovers and their second-time-around women, thighs touching thighs, the crazy sun in their eyes.

It's always black magic, isn't it? No, black isn't the colour. Try: mangoes, the underside of a parrot's wing, the nightly swelling of a tree frog's throat.

That search for something too late.

At home there is only snow.

It isn't really the sudden rain, the high wind, the careening drive around the island to Governor's Bay, the jerking mini-moke and the quick snap of my neck. The moke hit a patch of washed-out road. The sign read: WATCH FOR FALLING ROCK. PROCEED AT YOUR OWN RISK. He says the moke feels like a bumper car at the Exhibition. He says, *I'm General Patton*, after drinking four rum punches before dinner, a bottle of wine during, and several liqueurs after. It isn't the sudden rain.

It's never the place. It isn't really the wind sweeping the flowers off the table in our outside kitchen. No light in that cubby-hole. The cupboard doors won't snap shut and the wind whips them open so the corners crack the side of my head. No, it's never the place.

Something new. He brings me coffee after his French lesson with Solange. I think she makes him do that. Then she teaches me. The secret is to feel the emotion behind the language, within the new words. To talk with your hands and body. Solange is part Swedish, part French. Wide round face and golden skin. Flashing dense brown eyes. What made me cry was the rose. One yellow rose. He said Solange thought it was for her and gushed and fussed in French so he had to give it to her. You know how they are, he said, the French. I know. Someone new.

When you think of falling, you do. This afternoon we dared the long climb around the mountain from Anse des Flamands to La Petite Anse through thick underbrush and sea-washed caves. The wind pushed me against rock walls. The sea heaved on the shore far beneath me. When you think of falling, you do. Every exposed root, every footfall, reminding me of the lovely walk along the riverbank with you that noon, how I nested for a moment in a hollow, found my perch there, unafraid of the tumble-down. Now, I touched honeycombed rock, saw ancient heads and faces sculpted in them by the sea. I understood why the primitives believed in gods, in a power they could not control. I found shelter from a sudden shower inside a wide but shallow cave. I watched him watching naked lovers romp in the sea. I wished I could show you the seven waterfalls in Maui, the royal birthing caves. When you think of falling there — don't.

Why don't you? demands the answer: Because. He passes out after dinner. My sleep is strange here; I've never awakened in the dark of night before. You woke me up so abruptly I felt you had been beside me, on my left side, wearing your glasses. Why didn't you stay?

Are you waiting to see which way I will go, and when?

From a distance, Anse de L'Orient looks like a pubic triangle, the sea forming the base, the mountain peaks the top. At the crossroads, turbo-prop planes dive between the mountains, buffeted by crosswinds.

Languishing, nude, on the sand, I thought of a new job. A small apartment. It's wonderful what fresh flowers will do to a dark corner. I knew what books, paintings, I would take with, what I would leave that's his.

Along the shore, small bushes crawled: wide leaves, large green pods hard now and bursting, roots weaving in and out of themselves and the sand. Leafing out. One small purple flower. I plucked a pod but left the flower on its branch.

Then I walked the beach alone. The women were all middle-aged, breasts pulled down by too many suckling mouths. Why won't mine take the sun? The rest of me slowly turns golden. I felt like a silky petal about to fall from its stem. And just as I was thinking that the only way to forget is to find someone else and how surely you will find a blonde on your beach in Maui, I passed a curly-headed Latin digging in the sand with his infant daughter. Sunlight glinted on the airfield; a departing piper cut lifted off where the runway ends and the beach begins. Swimmers ducked, or dove deep.

I only saw you, floating down, without need of an oxygen tank, drifting past Hawaiian blue parrotfish, rainbow butterflyfish, whiteline triggerfish. Falling, deeper, into a submerged volcano, an inverted funnel of lava rock.

Far down the beach, the sea spume so warm on my legs, the sun pullied me behind the base of the mountain. I intended never to return.

Lord, I was so strong.

I turned back, finally, where a new dock extends out to sea.

When I reached the Latin again, his dark daughter ran crying to her mother. He offered me the purple flower. He actually bowed. Then spun around on one toe, and ambled back to his family.

I wouldn't have accepted the unnamed flower. I intended never to return.

Tree frogs don't sing for me here.

Here, in the corner of a small rock wall enclosing a fish pond, quiet and still, a tree frog hides beneath a flowering shrub. I knew I'd find one, and I wasn't even looking. Crouched, I wait for its throat to swell, the membrane white and gleaming in the moonlight.

It looks like it's made of marzipan, like the one you bought for me in a bakery once. Green coat fading, it still squats on top of my computer at the office, its chocolate base stuck to the shelf, its eyes turned upward, its pink tongue thrust out, mocking.

I'm waiting for its song.

I know what I will do when I return.

At home there is only snow.

◆◆◆

Doctor Dave:
> You win. I tried writing in the first person, just for you, but not *to* you. Yes, it's for Christophe — if he were here — and for you. Paul and I will have the whole summer together. At home.

Estelle.
– Winter, 1989
St. Bartheleme

PENETRATION ROCK

A great slab of lava lay at the bottom of the bay.

He dove down, kicking. He swam through the opening of the cave, surfaced and was immediately blinded by a heavy, dense fog. He reached up, kicked up, treading water, and the fog evaporated. He turned in a circle. He was enclosed by golden rock, walls rough and sculpted by once-hot lava. Behind him, the opening to the cave, and the sea sighed, the cold air moving in with the waves, turning to steam, washing back out with the departing wave. The cave breathed.

The incoming waves forced the water level inside the cave to rise, then fall as the waves retreated.

He dove, down, on a funnel of light, small blue and gold fish flitting before him. An octopus swung from a wedge of rock wall, a giant spider, the melting mist its web. The light faded as he descended, and he lost colours: first orange and red, then purple. Flipping his fins, arms reaching for the bottom, he floated down, deeper, deeper, past fish feeding. The net bag tied around his right wrist trailed along, inflated with water. Ahead, the great rock, impenetrable. Hearts and flowers and names carved on its surface. He dove, deeper, deeper.

Before he touched bottom, he kicked down, curled like a foetus, then legs cycling, and turning, he grasped the layered edge of the lava. He swept around, studying every notch, peering at black sea urchins, yellow spikes stiffening, a warning. Hands sweeping the flat surface now, bubbles rising, the tank lighter on his back. He checked his diving regulator: more than enough oxygen left. He brushed away sharp and crusted shale from the top of the rock, fingers seeking a crack in the rockbed.

His right foot sank and dark silt rose up, swirled around him, then rose towards the stronger light above him. He pushed, the seas's floor soft and yielding, and his flipper disappeared under the rock. He pulled it out, gripped the edge of the slab, knelt, groping.

He freed the net bag around his wrist, removed something blue and feathery and soft and slid it under the rock.

The rising, slowly, floating back to the surface.
The cave breathed.
The sea sighed.
Her name.

❖❖❖

Dave:

> In Maui I went scuba diving with Paul. Tonight, I dream of Christophe — he left my blue spirit under a great, unmovable lava rock. Don't fret. When you see it the canvas will take your breath away.

> Estelle.
> – March, 1990
> Hawaii

VI

WHERE DREAMS CANNOT RISE TO MORNING

He loved only the thing beyond his reach:
the part of the canal that disappears underground,
caves beneath the river,
the deepest part of his sleep
where dreams cannot rise to morning.

11. *La Maison Fell*
c. 1972
38.2 x 46 cm
Mackenzie Art Gallery, Regina

The only painting done from a central perspective and the only one in which Christophe appears as the artist at work, it was apparently done, hastily, on the morning of the Carons' last day in Provence, just hours before Christophe's leap from Pont du Gard.

The medieval fieldstone house, with its vaulted ceilings, summer and winter kitchens, open hearths, spiral interior staircases and stone exterior stairways has thick walls that keep it cool in the dry hot summer. From the exterior, the centre of the house looks like a chimney, with square blocked annexes added at odd angles. A stone wall that extends beyond the house encloses a garden of mulberry, cypress, plane and olive trees, and the viewer can almost hear the buzz and saw of crickets, which Caron described as "electric, like the fervour of a mosquito zapper gone berserk or a multitude of underground water sprinklers spinning out of control." Beyond the wild sun-scorched grasses, cultivated sunflower fields sweep toward rolling tunnels of lavender; the manic movement reminiscent of Van Gogh is created by pin-point splashes of red ochre.

Set deep into the stone walls, shutterless windows are barred but open to the Provencal light. And, in each one the head and bare shoulders of a young girl appears, each one Estelle Caron at ages varying from thirteen to her then age of twenty-one. Her hair is shoulder length, centre parted, the colour and texture of straw. The age of each is determined by lengthening shadows in the face, ranging from a pale yellow to a deep olive to dark grey, with a mottled effect like the bark of the plane tree. Odd-angled crevices, slits and genital-like apertures are cut into mortar and stone and tree trunks. Projected bonding-stones, inverted arches, and round cover slabs not found in photographs she took of the house in 1972 suggest the Pont du Gard painting that Estelle Caron would work on for the next twenty years. The house, which so clearly blends with the Provencal landscape, was built from its earthworks and fieldstone, and critics — even those who vehemently reject Freudian theories — may acknowledge the house-as-woman motif in this painting because of Caron's artistic associative leap to the troubadour theme of the damsel imprisoned in a tower.

Unusual cloud formations above the house hold hints of swirling, untamed beards, arched noses nudging between swelling breast shapes, *Monts de Venus*, and Rubens-like hips and thighs.

While time is at once dissolved yet integrated through the miniature portraits of Estelle at each window, this is the only painting which contains only one story, one central character and theme.

It is not so surprising, given the tragic event of their last day in Lussan, that it foretells the Canadian prairie story-paintings of figure and landscape that later broke through all restrained and realistic prairie themes and folk art of her century.

12. Where Dreams Cannot Rise to Morning
(Regina, Christmas, 1991)

How does a mother convey to her son his father's frustrations, his insecurities, his sexuality?

You must read, read and then read more. Try to understand the Catholic madonna and whore complex, the courtly love of ancient times, how obsessed your father was with these, not merely because of his monastic upbringing, his early years in a boys' school in Marseille.

He only loved the thing beyond his reach: the part of the canal that disappears underground, caves beneath the river, the deepest part of sleep where dreams cannot rise to morning.

For so many years, I blamed myself for his death. I had disappointed him. I could never be the mother he wanted for you. I failed to reach him at the other end of the aqueduct though I called and called. Because he was so gentle so sensitive so kind a lover before we were married I didn't know until too late about the *other*, or what prompted such rage, though bits of it I caught in the sketches and drawings: the feather, the claw, the cloven hoof.

WOMAN FROM SONG

From the moon you can see the stone wall around the house. Hear the mingling of two rivers where a massive bridge spans green waters. There, I find river ducks, my will to go on without you abandoned to the scrutiny. The drake sheds his bright feathers for a dull eclipse of plumage, shaking his head and whistling while the female nests. She tries to incubate a clutch of cracked eggs. Breeding done, they can't fly.

Across the bridge, your shadow casts on water. You must want to know about our son. I can only tell you of the music he composes and about his flight. I don't know where he is, if he's safe. Arms pinned and heavy as wet wings, in this, my moulting season, there is no comfort, no changing.

On the rainbow bridge, a Swedish sun-maid waits, astride a cloud horse. She wears a golden neck ring and amber rings, the stones of the sun, tears of the Tree. Once, she cracked bones with hot stones and foretold the future from the lines. She said a drink from the Springs of Mimir would give knowledge of events to come. But the oracle lies in Baltic amber, in sun stones, the World Tree tears. She lifts her arm, her mother-call a new offering:
    We may look back.
    From the moon.

❖❖❖

(I found this prose-poem among my mother's notes, unsigned and undated, but it must have been written in Regina, the summer of 1988 when I ran away to Vancouver and didn't contact her for five days. Then only sixteen, I was into heavy metal, motorcycles, dope, and a headstrong determination to flee my father's ghost and find

my own destiny. When I ran out of money I sold my motorcycle. The RCMP found me busking at the Granville Island Market, and sent me home on the bus. It was the kind of wild, headstrong act so typical of my father, and it was that realization — more than the consequences any punishment could have achieved — together with my mother's suffering that whirled me around and brought me to an abrupt halt. I returned to school to please my mother. P. C.)

CHAINED TO THE RAILING OF THE STEPS
THAT LEAD UP TO THE WALL OF HIGH ART

When she was young he sent her his religious poetry, words sculpted deep in pages that read from bottom to top, and she wrote back: try a new form. Years later, she doesn't know why she has finally come here to the home of his youth. She has never before seen this white house, its picketed yard, the shrouded spruce. Inside, she waits. She has done this before: aproned and patient, cooked his last meal in clay pots. His golden child crayons, a sun-bleached table. When he arrives the boy cannot see him. His white hair will never grow back. He has no eyebrows. He has willed her here. With wrist-cuff and chain, he binds her to the railing of the steps that lead up to the towering wall of art so high above her she cannot even see the tower to the sky, to the light of the moon.

♦♦♦

D.L.K.:
    He's home. Safe.
    This morning, Paul said, "Why can't you be like other mothers and bake bread?" This story is my answer to him — and to you. My comfort when I call.

E.G.C.
– August 29, 1988
Regina

THE DRAFT DODGER, THE FLOWER CHILD, THE IBEX

When he was a baby he was knocked from his mother's hip by an angry goat and he's been tetched in the head ever since.

He never learned to walk upright; he leaps and bounds in the goat meadow on all fours.

He cannot talk. He snuffles and snorts. Bites the baby goats' ears. Runs at his mother hanging washing on the line and butts her belly with his head. When she picks him up he scratches her arms.

His father is a draft dodger, his mother a flower child. They raise Angoras in the long valley between mountains.

At night the boy lies on his cot under the window, batting the screen with the back of his hand. He yowls at the moon while Nana rocks. She has stopped tending the goats, no longer sheers their long fleece, no longer tans hides for shoes, gloves. She rocks, weeping.

Abraham pares his fingernails with a skinning knife, chews the inside of his cheeks, chuffing.

The boy points at the window, at the moon riding the crest of the mountain. He howls.

And the Ibex appears on the sudden edge of the sky, head uplifted. Horns.

The boy bangs his head against the screened window.

He's out there, Abraham says. The boy knows.

Nana spits out the taste of rancid goat cheese. We never should have come here, she says.

She lifts the boy, he wraps his hind legs around her thin hips. She walks him, patting his back, stroking his sweat-soaked hair.

Abraham ties his long hair back with a leather thong. He picks up his Bible, opens it, words blurring. I'll kill that cloven-foot devil, he says.

He plans a sneak attack from the side or behind. He stalks the Ibex up the switchback where waters divide, watching for signs: an empty wolf den, bleached elk or moose bones, blood spoor. He sights the Bighorn in single file along the ridgeline beyond the perpetual snow. Two bucks square off, rear, run at each other, hides and muscles rippling along arched backs. When their horns hit the mountain booms and echoes. Abraham listens to the night-long howl of his son, Nana's sudden cry. The goats back away, dazed, eyes rolling, noses bleeding. Charge again. The C-R-A-C-K of bone on bone, that echo again. Abraham leaps from one rock shelf to another. He huddles against the side of a ledge.

Snow blows over him.

And Nana, the boy with the surly temper and short upturned tail on her hip.

The mound of snow trembles.

And the Ibex rises up.

Every night it butts the boy out of his mother's arms.

◆ ◆ ◆

Dr. Keening:
    Freud was wrong. And so are you. Dreams are not wish-fulfillments. Stories are dreams realized. I cannot know what mine mean, though I'm so afraid of losing Paul. The son too much like his father.

Estelle Gunnerson Caron.
– January 1, 1989
(Likely Banff, Alberta – P.C.)

WHITE HORSE PEOPLE

She was the first woman, and he was the stranger who came riding, riding.

She was the first turf-artist. Long haired, wild and free. She cut the turf herself, deep in the Down, a way-marker, a signature: her name, his.

There was no village on the Down then, no high priest to shame her, she who only loved and lost and lived to create the first white horse, deep in the Down. He said he was off to hunt again, the solstice would bring him back with plenty of meat and game for her father, her mother, and the child she would bear him in the spring.

She waited, her patience as old as the pale moon, its pull. When it yielded to the new sun, still wrapped in tanned sheepskin, she squatted before the fire outside her thatched-roof hut, gazing — up — at the long slope of the dragon-headed, hunchbacked hills, following the long line — down — to the farther slope to the south. She watched the light lift and break and fall and rise again, then fold down on the way he had first come to her and would again.

She had no doubt that he would return.

Every morning, she watched. Waited. With a stick, she poked and scraped at the hoof-turned turf, the green of the grass clutched in her hand. She tugged and turned the scarred earth: white, radiant, chalky. She etched the lifted head of a reined-in steed, its white eye rolling.

With each new light, the promised sight of him grew stronger, the horse and rider, bearing down, moving forward, the kick of the child hard within her.

The solstice came and went, and still she waited, now suckling the newborn girlchild. He would come, yes he would come to her. When three more solstices had come and gone again, and the child tottered after spring lambs and the grass yellowed and withered, wanting rain, it was time to move south to new grounds. She dug her dirty toes into the turf and refused to move, overcome with the vision of her horseman charging down, his yellow hair flapping against his shoulders, a lanky forelock swept back from dense brown eyes, but he would fail to see her. Then he would search but never find her.

She had no doubt that he would come. Something had delayed him, but no matter what had befallen him, as long as he was alive, he would someday someway find a way to return.

I must leave a mark, she said. She drew a horse in the chalk, its nose pointing south, its tail lifted and flowing behind. Her father huffed and grunted. Her mother stirred the stewed lamb and said, Let her leave a sign for him, the direction he must follow, saying with downcast eyes that the father must help to the task. And when it was done they could strike out for new feeding grounds.

Then she began her life's work.

Once he reached Dragon Hill, he would know, yes he would see from the long line of shank and rump and curved back how steadfast her love, her waiting, wanting. And when he saw the elongated nose and the direction it pointed towards he would know which way to go to find her and his child. Spurring on his steed, he would hasten to them.

She sent her father to the lowland. From Dragon Hill, she pointed out the design, laying it out from a distance: the faraway lines of legs and back and arching neck, drawing the white horse in miniature. With a sheering stone, she cut the outline for him there. And when he stooped at the appointed place to start, she began to wave and shout and point, while he marked the spots with wooden pegs, connecting them with sinew strings until it was clearly marked: the shape of running horse.

Then together they began, digging, turning the turf, a trench two feet deep, baring the white chalk.

Several suns passed over the Downs, several moons illuminated the outline, but even then she was not satisfied. The entire horse must be cut and filled with chalk.

And they ceased forever their nomadic wandering. Her mother planted corn, wild onions, turnips.

It took seven years to finish. And when it was done she stood in the horse's eye with her own eyes shut, turned three times and made the wish.

Then she and her father ventured a little distance, looked back and surveyed the Down.

It began to rain, that grey drizzle that lowers the sky and casts shadows over the land.

The horse. The great white beast, with its running legs, as thin and disjointed as the weeping woman who left her waymarker for her lover to follow, faced east. Slowly it shifted, the chalk flowing into wet earth.

Stone deaf, her father had failed to hear her directions from so far. He cut a *V* between the ears, severed the forelock from the neck, the high brow and wattled jaws, the nose too much like a beak, or no, it was her nose, turned down.

She sank to her knees. The rain and its gradual erosion would drop the horse by degrees, lower its tail until it flowed between his legs. A long-eared, bony dog.

The turf crawls while man sleeps, her father said.

She lifted her head, let him take her elbow and raise her to her feet.

Look again, he said.

The smooth curves of back and neck slowly blended with the line and flow of the hillside, with the line and flow of her love. The horse was solid. White. One large round eye, a weeping eye. The grass grew upward from the bottom and fell curving from the top.

The horse began to move uphill.
And the rider descended.

◆◆◆

Paul Dear:
    Looking to my father's side of the family, I discovered our first ancestor: a turf-artist. I dream her nightly so I can paint *The White Horse* for you. The horseman will look like your father, my love from afar.

(No date. Unsigned. P.C.)

RAGNAROK

She kept the sun-chaser Wolf from the door of her last winter house.

While it tried to swallow an old sun, the Swedish grandmother preserved raspberries, put tomatoes up in jars. Beside her tin and nickel stove she stacked poplar chips in boxes, seasoned logs.

Here is her wintergreen salve, her smelling salts. Her sun hat hangs forgotten on a peg nailed into the shingled wall. Here are her sweet mints, an orange, her small comforts. Now the grandmother is gone, who will hold the family together? keep the wolf from the door? Now the grandmother is gone, her mother returns to the one-room, sun-shingled house.

She finds her when the sun falls behind the slanted roof. She finds her looking into the house through the single eye of the single window. Her hair is vibrant, marcelled. She finds her there, no older than the day she ran away. She doesn't ask, Why did you leave me? Why have you come back now? There are a hundred years between them.

There are a hundred years between the grandmother and the mother, between her and another young beauty behind her, the daughter she will never have, perhaps.

The child wears the raspberry silk dressing gown the mother left behind. She doesn't look like any woman in the family, her hair so long so free.

The mother doesn't say, I was the first one, the only one who got out. She doesn't say, I have come for you, we'll run away, this time together. She tells her daughter to bob her hair, she's too old for braids and ribbons. The mother leads her daughter into the house, leaving the granddaughter she is determined never to have outside, wanting in, perhaps. The screened door complains.

WHERE DREAMS CANNOT RISE TO MORNING

The springs of the old bed, coiled, shriek with their sinking weight. The mother and daughter do not touch. Their burnished hair glints in the slant of an old light, rays of a dying sun. No, they do not touch. They hear the wolfhound's long howl, hear it stir under the grandmother's bed. The great animal heaves and crawls out, leaps upon the bed, between mother and daughter, this enormous wolfdog that hauled the mother's sled three miles down the railway tracks to the one-room schoolhouse. It leans, heavy upon the daughter, against her raised knees. It lifts its shaggy head, yellow teeth bared. It's jaws snap. It snarls. It's eye rolls back and she sees in that third eye the ship of the sun, its flight from Wolf around the World Tree. She calls her mother's name, afraid.

— And so you should be, the mother says. She wraps and twists the grandmother's dish-towel around the pointed snout, a sun-bleached muzzle. She ties it tight so Wolf cannot bite or swallow.

— He is Wolf, the mother says. The Wolf that pursues the ship of the sun. After the last battle it will swallow the sun.

And winter will cover the earth.

❖ ❖ ❖

Dave:
    This morning my mother left us. She didn't know Paul or me at the end. Who is the unwanted child? Not me, surely, the only daughter.

                                    Estelle.
                             – Winter, 1989
                                Saskatoon

VII

BEYOND THE *COUILLARDE*

I sensed an approaching touch, *promising an emergence, an opening as if a metal door into a mountain were about to swing wide and reveal to me an inner truth: the dark side of light. And that revelation, as old as allegories, folktales, myths and magic could only come to me where midnight black can change to grey to blue to azure.*

13. *Morning At Pont du Gard*
c. 1972-1992
73 x 92 cm.
Private Collection, Paul Caron

No one knows which of the hundreds of sketches and studies were done in the early hours of the Carons' last morning at Lussan. All of them are signed, but not all are dated.

Here, for want of space, I can only include two sketches she prepared before the final approach to the canvas.

In the first, *The Hare* (cat. figure 21), drawn with strong serpentine charcoal curves, and long laboured strokes of olive-green paint, Estelle portrays her husband with Medusa-like hair and the now familiar bird-claw hands and feet, rearing back in terror before an emerging watersprite with ochre-red bruises about bulbous hips and breasts. With one hand, she hides her sex in the Venus pose, and from it trail lavender stocks. His satchel has fallen to the ground and from it spill limestone chips with various impressions of phallic symbols similar to the Hare/Gopher found on Pont du Gard. In an attempt to ward her off, in a striking pose, he raises a three-pronged Gardien's trident, bearing the flag of St. George slaying the dragon.

In the second sketch, an acrylic study (cat. figure 22), titled *Reincarnation*, the artist depicts the building of the Pont; Christophe in red tunic, on the highest arch, checking the levels with the Chorobate, and directing the movement of the squirrel cage, a wooden-wheeled apparatus that lifts giant slabs with pulleys and winch to the top of the third arch.

BEYOND THE *COUILLARDE*

The highest aqueduct built by the Romans, the Pont du Gard consists of three superimposed arches made of masonry blocks, each slab weighing six tons. The final painting of my father on the top, viewed from the odd perspective of the passageway, with none of the massive arches or river below in view, shows the walkway made of roofing slabs; it transverses from bank to bank and looks like a carriage way suspended and curving over the top of the trees.

Unclothed, with shorts, canvas hat and backpack carefully set to one side, Christophe is seen from behind, his hairy haunches curving Pan-like down to cloven feet. He peers into an entrance to the aqueduct canal that looks like the tunnelled opening to a dungeon or tomb. His legs are spread in a crouch position and between them hangs the enlarged stone phallus of the Roman engineer.

In an azure cloudless sky, to the northeast, his spirit (painted finally in 1992) takes flight in the form of a blue mythological figure who is half eagle, half man. The feathered head with its yellow hooked beak turns in profile, as the gigantic wings spread over the tree-tops.

He soars towards a cold moon.

14. The Night of the Fall
   (La Maison Fell, June, 1992)
   (*Twenty years later*)

For five weeks I had tried but failed to comfort him or lift him out of his depression. I was searching for the nude in the landscape and I suddenly had become my own muse; I saw my own blue spirit reclining in a tunnel of lavender, languishing among leaves, calling to Christophe, but he couldn't see *me*. Not even in the bath or Lussan boudoir. Though his passion was never spent and I believed I was easily satisfied, I awoke each morning feeling so — alone.

And then I began to imagine that, now his *amour de longh* was over, brought into the hard light with its consummation, he searched for a new great-love-at-a-great-distance. Strolling through village streets, at curb-side cafés, those black eyes wandered, and he leered — at waitresses, students at nearby tables, swimmers and sunbathers: all the nymphs.

And so it was, as we made our way along the highest arch of the aqueduct, your father searched wildly — silently — for the phallus engraved in the slabstone. All along the riverside, in its shallow pools, and on every walkway and arch bathers absorbed the high sun. Except for North American tourists, the women were half nude.

I wore a peasant skirt and poor-boy sleeveless top, and though I wasn't counted among the bra-burning women's libbers of the decade, it was simply too hot for underwear.

Christophe stopped to fix his wild, intense stare on a blonde, nubile German tourist who lay upon a roof slab dragged away from the ragstone vault of the canal, her round, rosy face lifted and eyes closed like a sun worshipper. He shrugged out of the backpack containing the heavy iron groma used in antiquity for sighting. He knelt on one knee, and without thinking I said, "Oh, Chris, you're staring at breasts again."

And then he was no longer your father, rising up, satchel in hands rough and worn from scrabbling through shale and underground vaults; he hurled the heavy canvas sack at me, striking me hard in the belly. I caught it like a leather gymnastic medicine ball, hunched over, my breath lost more with fear than from the blow.

He whirled into a kind of frenzied dance, as if possessed by Bacchus, spinning and flitting from edge to edge of the walkway. He shouted, *"Fini! Fini!"* His red-rimmed eyes glared, his nostrils flared, cheeks bulged in fury, teeth bared. And he yelled, "I've had it with you, you do nothing but criticize, nothing pleases you, you never laugh, and it's over, done, never again, *Ça c'est tout!"* I dropped the back-pack, he caught it up and dashed it onto the slab, shouting in French and Latin and Italian, a stunning jumble as if he were speaking in tongues, words I couldn't understand, except for the name, Pliny the Elder. He wheeled closer, closer, then gripped my arm. His fingernails tore the skin inside my elbow.

When he released me I retreated backwards, slowly, dangerously close to the edge, then froze there as if I would never move again, like a pillared reinforcement spur to divide the river current.

If I didn't move I wouldn't be struck, but if I did I might release us. Slowly, I lifted my yellow shirt, exposing rounded belly first, then freed breasts, and let it fall down my bronzed arms. Then I flung it into the air. Caught by an updraught from the canal vault below, it lifted and whirled like an unfurled ship's flag, and floated down, towards the river.

I lifted my head, squared my shoulders, and strode down the passageway, beyond him, expecting him to follow, humbled, sorry, with promises never to hurt me again.

And then I heard the cry, the girl's not his, and shouts from the lower arches and from the riverbed. I turned around and was stopped by the sight of his great leap: arms pinned to his sides, feet tight together, the body a dark and curving line, parallel to the slant of the sun, the high pillared arch.

And then gone.

WE HAVE COME TO THIS

Without love, there can be no story.

It has to open and close with this: If I could see you today and tell you all, this is the story I would give you.

There are others. Those who once drove by tree-enclosed asylum grounds, who accelerated with fear, or slowed with the thrill of the unknown and loved the anticipation of danger as if a ghost story were told late at night. They still believe in something impossible, not probable.

I want to reach those who told me to give up, to throw you out, as if you chose to be different.

And I believed those who said if I let you go you would learn to look after yourself; I had to give you that chance, that independence. Yet here I am dining on *canard* at Le Tour d'Argent while you must still be contemplating stealing a jar of peanut butter and bread from a confectionary. When I told your social worker no one can live on $40 per week and I would call the media if you were pushed to that he said, "This isn't Jean Val Jean." And then he threatened to cut you off if he caught me giving you anything more than a gift at Christmas. "I step over people like your son every morning on my way to work," he said. "All he needs is some old fashioned bum-kicking."

When you were born I believed that all one had to give to a child was love; and if I could undo the past, return to that beginning, and if it were possible to give you only one gift, it would be this story.

I had so little confidence of my own then, and your father had barely enough for himself, having to prove himself every time he designed a new bridge or built a road.

And then he was gone, even before you were born.

I want the part about love to be true.

I need to believe in that power to heal.
Let hope return.

To: St. Germain de Près and L'Hotel Marronniers on the Left Bank. A garden of chestnut trees surrounded by glass walls. A small red landscape by Bruegel on the pillar opposite the reception desk. A lift so small it holds only the Canadian woman's luggage, easel, and boxes of paints.

Swiftly, she climbs the carpeted stairs that encircle the slow-moving lift and slant like a tower staircase.

Room 51. As small as a cell. Pressed styrofoam walls she is compelled to touch to believe in. A single lamp, plastic vines with electric candles. A wooden desk, leather chair. A two-drawer chest. A double bed, French linen. One dormer window opening over the courtyard and garden of chestnuts. Garrets. Chimney pots. Pigeons.

Here, visitors pay dearly for old and charming.

And then it begins. So fast so fleeting. The walls become plaster, cracked. The oak floor is covered with stained indoor-outdoor carpeting. The antique furniture is replaced by a Sally Ann chesterfield and chair. The bed vanishes and she almost falls onto the foam mattress. She is ankle deep in cigarette butts, paper scraps, jagged soup cans, crushed milk and juice cartons, and what's left of her son's clothing. He cannot — or will not? — look after himself. The sink is so corroded Comet cleanser cannot touch it. She opens the fridge: warm stale air. No food. A box of Kraft macaroni, scrambled egg scorched in a frying pan, a bent spoon and a cracked cup on the counter. Empty cupboards. He has hung an orange sheet over the window.

Just as she is about to unpack the groceries she brought the room rights itself.

She didn't see that.

She doesn't see a barrister. Not robed, not yet. A senior counsel for the defence. Grey fedora, grey coat over a red hand-knit sweater. Effeminate. Arrogant. He lifts his chin. *We shall not consult the family*, he says. And it happens again.

As fast as she can turn around, the dormer windows become French doors that open onto a balcony. White sheets hang like shrouds on the wooden railing. Flower pots. Red geraniums. A blond youth lies on a mat before the open double doors. His limbs are as white and perfect as the marble statues of Greek gods she saw in every museum, in every gallery, in Parisian parks. His head is not connected to his body. A woman in black lifts a bucket and pours water into a china basin.

And the artist suddenly *knows* that the youth was charged with crushing a flower. With stealing a loaf of bread.

He was innocent but condemned without trial.

He rises up from a mat before the French doors, reconnected, whole.

Still guilty.

Until proven innocent.

As swift as the falling blade of the guillotine, the room reorders itself, and she knows she didn't really see or hear anything, that she had a fleeting *sense* of something beyond her ears and eyes, of what did or did not happen in this room. She calls the concierge and makes a reservation for dinner. She tries not to think about her son, about his father's fear of the unknown but certain day of his falling. Of brain disorder. Of misunderstanding.

Tomorrow she will visit the place where Marie Antoinette, Danton and Robespierre were held before being led to Place de la Concord and the guillotine. The executioner was called Monsieur de Paris.

To: La Conciergerie. Not a museum. Bars on the windows. Armed policemen. Gendarmes block the door. They shift and create a space between them, revealing a wooden table and a sign in English: DEPOSIT ALL METAL OBJECTS. The fair-haired security guard examines the contents of the woman's flightbag: a French/English dictionary, a makeup bag, passport, Edith Piaff compact disc and a miniature Damian print she bought this morning. The pimple-faced gendarme frisks her with his metal detector, passing it over and under her raised arms.

And they let her go.

Inside, the courthouse looks like a cathedral: high vaulted windows, marble stairways. To the left, a small courtroom that may have once been a chapel, the altar now the judges' bench. Massive oiled walnut panels. Pews. High windows with bars instead of stained glass, open to street noise and yellow light paling between low grey clouds. Four prisoners in the dock, heads lifted; the last look at the sky.

She finds a free seat in the third row.

Lawyers. More of them than clients. All in black silks with wide satin sleeves, pleated court tabs that look like bibs. All young, bronzed. Women with hair tied in bows. Flirting, those flashing French eyes. Maybe making dates for dinner.

Without the birthright of a language, one must see more, sense everything.

In France, the accused are guilty until proven innocent. No jury box. A lower court, perhaps, similar to provincial courts in Canada. The Canadian woman assumes the trials are over, that the judgements and sentences are about to be handed down from the bench.

Everyone waits for the judges.

She begins to sketch. Behind each prisoner, a gendarme in black uniform sits upright with arms folded. Other blue-shirted policemen block the exits and entrances to the dock and to the courtroom.

The first prisoner, a swarthy youth with swollen lips, breathes through his open mouth; an asthmatic. The second, a blond boy in a yellow shirt, so tall so thin, pale skin, pointed teeth that cross and protrude. No money for braces. She wonders if he has impacted wisdom teeth. Someone must take her own son to the dentist. Large luminous eyes she swears she has seen before: vacant. Dark half-moon shadows imbedded under his eyes. So pale. He has lived in an institution. His left arm is rolled in a dirty bandage, cradled and held close to his chest. His hands are red as if he has held them in cold water too many hours each day; a butcher's helper or fishmonger in a market. Her son fell ill when he was seventeen with the same illness that felled her husband: manic flights to the moon and barometric drops deeper than the sea. He has never had a job. When a lawyer approaches the dock and whispers to the prisoner he holds his hands together as if in prayer. The lawyer tosses his hair over his shoulder, head swinging and gesturing towards a woman in the first row, the mother: the same overly-large nose, with flared nostrils. She has tried to hide her worn black coat with a red shawl tied across the shoulders. She lifts a gloved hand and reaches out, then grips the railing separating her from her son. Her shoulders hunch, tight, as if trying to pull her head into her neck. There is no father, no influences. "See," she says. "Love is not enough."

The prisoners look like a street gang, but they don't speak to each other. The sick boy drops his head onto his arms on the railing. The first boy, the swarthy newcomer, yawns. The other two prisoners fidget and stare at their feet.

All young, poor, uneducated, so in need of baths, good food, clean clothing. No one has shaved for days. No one has made them presentable for court. They look mean, tough, like criminals. The artist scribbles on the margin of her sketchpad: *They look guilty*.

An electric buzzer announces the judges' entrance. The first judge is so handsome the Canadian woman gasps and clamps her gloved hand over her mouth. Black curly hair, those dense French eyes, tanned cheeks that will turn to jowls after too many years of wine and *canard* at Le Tour d'Argent. She writes: *And he looks so clean so rested so well groomed*. The second judge is a woman, about forty, worn thin by her profession, its demands. Her dirty-blonde hair hangs in clumps. No makeup. Deep lines around her mouth from grinding her teeth in her sleep, no doubt. Grey skin, grey eyes. The Canadian woman resolves to cut her own hair, get more sleep, yell at the social worker instead of clenching her teeth. The last judge looks like a magistrate from any country: elderly, bespeckled, bald, with a monk's fringe.

The young, handsome judge shuffles long scrolls of paper on which he has made notes. No red hard-cover Q.B. notebook. He calls out each prisoner's number, delivers the judgement, sentences each one. And the policemen behind each prisoner rise and lead the convicted away; as each row of prisoners is sentenced, they are immediately replaced by new accused, new guards who look exactly like the last set.

Leaving the boy. The pale blond youth in a yellow shirt. Brown eyes. Black crooked teeth. He mouths words at his mother in the front row, desperate, afraid, perhaps angry. He chews dirty fingernails.

There but for an accident of conception.

When it's his turn, when his number is called, the judge looks at the blond boy with the same immobile face as if his emotions were bronzed by Damian.

And it happens again.

The courtroom dissolves itself and reemerges as a single-story concrete building, no windows. Mahogany panelling behind the judge's bench. A maple leaf flag. A mountie at attention beside the prisoner's box. One lawyer in Q.C. silks. A red sash appears around the judge's neck and shoulders. His hair thins, turns grey at the temples. Bifocals slip over his nose. The artist strains to hear unfamiliar words over the traffic noises mounting though the window. She hears the word: *leçon*. And then the pronouncements are paternal, in English: *Take responsibility for your illness. Take your medicine, don't cheek it then flush it down the toilet when the nurse has gone. Not so sick you can't go back to* school. *All in your head.* Then the words reshape themselves back into French, it is *leçon* she hears, the courtroom replaces itself here and now, in Paris. A number translates into years. And the blond boy wilts, shrivels, then *wafts* down; he faints. Two blue-shirts catch him under the arms and drag him out, head first through the door, his pigeon-toed feet scraping the floor.

The red-shawled woman cries out, and the blue-shirts move towards her. The handsome judge holds up his hand like a traffic cop. He says, *"Les mères, elles seront les mères."*

The Canadian artist rises, and before she emerges onto Quay Voltaire the old words begin:

— That won't happen to my boy!

In fiction, there doesn't have to be failure.
    In my story, the woman will go home.
    She will plant geraniums.
    Bake bread.

◆◆◆

(*Unmailed letter to Paul Caron. No date.*)

AFTERWORD

I approach the entrance to a 15th century dungeon descending, gradually, in seven levels.

No windows. Track lighting.

The walls are sand blasted and white washed, though prisoners' initials and dates in Roman numerals were etched as high as I can reach standing on tip-toe.

The floor is freshly lined with crushed, sea-bleached stone.

This is the Volti Galley in the old fortress at Ville Franche Sur La Mer. Where my mother often sought solitude, dream time, inspiration.

Next month, the opening for the audience only I desired for her, perhaps.

Twenty years in the making, I can only hope that the completion of the portrait of Christophe Emile Caron at Pont du Gard finally ended the artist's search for her husband's eternal *amour de longh* just prior to her death in a car accident on the Grande Cornishe above Côte d'Azure in 1992.

The details of her death are far less important than the legacy of art, but suffice it to say that she was returning to La Maison Fell after a brief holiday here, in Ville Franche Sur La Mer, when she was caught in a tragic game of "leapfrog" played by two truckers. A careful driver, my mother always stayed in the slow lane. Ahead, two trucks repeatedly passed each other, first one, then the other, and the first again, their steam whistle, a harbinger she could not have failed to hear. She swung out, into the middle lane, and passed the second one, but couldn't gain enough speed to overtake the first. The last truck accelerated, moved into the middle lane, shoving her red Peugot into the fast lane where the car was crushed between an oncoming moving van and the truck. The coroner said she would have died almost instantly.

I am now compelled to repeat that I found over two hundred studies, sketches and paintings in the Lussan house she rented each summer alone, together with more than a thousand pages of notes in a loosely bound portfolio depicting her struggles to understand the complexities of her husband's character and recreate the event for me.

So afraid, all her life, that I would be struck by the same illness that drove my father to finally take his own life, she believed in the preventative and therapeutic value of art.

I cannot agree.

I no longer believe that my father's death, that singular leap from the magestic aqueduct, was the driving force behind my mother's art, or that when she signed her name to the final portrait she was healed. How often she said or wrote to me: "I live for art. There is nothing more important."

There were, of course, other people in Estelle Caron's life, some brief appearances of a lover in Montserrat or the French island of St. Barthelme, a few lasting friendships with other artists, but mostly the wandering artist was attracted to the bag lady, the street artists in Nice, the backwoods people and the haunted folk. Perhaps that's why I chose the academic world, another kind of retreat into the mindscape.

If my father had lived to build a bridge over the North Saskatchewan River and they had settled in an ordinary split-level house somewhere in Saskatoon, conceived more children, my mother, the artist, would have followed the light that took her to exotic places and would have found all the nudes in the landscapes. She may have been absorbed in a quest for the father who died before she was born, a sub-theme of her work.

AFTERWORD

And now, surveying the exhibition the night before the opening, I look beyond the hidden light in each and every portrait of my father and there:
The artist.
My mother.

– Paul Caron
Ville Franche Sur La Mer
June 1, 1996

BIBLIOGRAPHY

1. Carpenter, D. Cameron. *Floating Eden*. Five Bridges Press: Saskatoon, 1972.

2. Binns, Loie A. *Falling for the Moon: Women Who Love Too Much*. Five Bridges Press: Saskatoon, 1980.

3. Vanderhead, Margaret. *Dancing with Herod: An Artist's Choice*. BlueMoon Publishers Ltd.: Wadena, 1990.

4. Patrick, L. *The Animal Inside*. Crowfoot Press: Calgary, 1969.

5. Virgil, S. *Loving Beyond the Grave*. University of Dublin Press: Dublin, 1985.

6. Tremblay, Fafard. *A Cow on Every Lawn: Changing Art for Changing Women*. Pile '0 Hides Publishers: Regina, 2000.

7. Keening, Dr. D.L. *Kissing the Blarney Stone: The Lies We Tell Our Children*. Moose Mouth Press: Moose Jaw, 1989.

8. Weissenheimer, Emmanuel G., Phd. "The Cézannic Fear of Women". *Psychology Tomorrow*. Volume 13: 108-200.